SAMUEL R. DELANY
has taken you
through strange and wonderful
worlds of the imagination
in his science-fiction
bestsellers
Nova,
Dhalgren,
Triton,
and
Tales of Neverÿon.

Journey now through a
vanished world
of youthful joy
and extraordinary dreams . . .
The real life story
of a brilliant writer
told as only he can tell it.

HEAVENLY BREAKFAST
An Essay on the Winter of Love

Heavenly Breakfast

An Essay on the
Winter of Love

by
Samuel R. Delany

BANTAM BOOKS
TORONTO · NEW YORK · LONDON

HEAVENLY BREAKFAST
AN ESSAY ON THE WINTER OF LOVE
A Bantam Book/September 1979

ISBN 0-553-12796-9

Published simultaneously in the United States and Canada

Bantam Books are published by Bantam Books, Inc. Its trade-
mark, consisting of the words "Bantam Books" and the por-
trayal of a bantam, is Registered in U.S. Patent and Trademark
Office and in other countries. Marca Registrada. Bantam
Books, Inc., 666 Fifth Avenue, New York, New York 10019.

PRINTED IN THE UNITED STATES OF AMERICA

This book is dedicated
to everyone who ever
did anything
no matter how sane or crazy
whether it worked or not
to give themselves
a better life.

We are ourselves the entities to be analyzed.

—Heidegger *Being and Time*

THE WINTER OF LOVE

We near an even dozen years from the incidents contouring these reflections. In the summer of 1967, the phrase-happy media, looking over San Francisco's young-folk and the Bay-area's emergent rock groups ("Moby Grape," "Big Brother and the Holding Company," "Country Joe and the Fish" . . .), dubbed it all the Summer of Love. But whatever process was caught in crosssection by the image glimmering around the phrase (a barefoot adolescent of nonspecific gender, standing in Golden Gate Park and holding a flower, wearing not much and that mostly handmade), the process was finally too complex for the image to cover.

Nowhere in that image, for instance, can one see even a shadow of the murder of Martin Luther King by James Earl Ray; or the failed murder attempt of Andy Warhol by Valery Solanas—knocked off the front page a day later with the murder of Robert Kennedy by Sirhan Sirhan; or the black students' occupying the halls of Columbia University and the night-long police brutalities that ended the incident and began a wave of like incidents in universities across the country. All images the year following that summer were to fit around the sunny picture, to keep it in place, to give it proportion. That sunny image is only the most palatable sign for the process that the others sign as well: the radical revisions going on in our model of the relation of human being to human being across each individual's personal political space: female to male, male to female, black to white, white to black, private individual to politicized group, or group to individual.

The truth is, of course, that despite any image, which, however briefly, served as its sign, the process had been going on for a long time. It is still going on, still moves us, moves among us, no matter how its look, its tenor, or its terms change.

This essay concerns a situation that is, both in historical time and sociological space, only a frame away from that summer image (1967 was the first year I heard people claim Haight-Ashbury was just a suburb of the East Village . . . or vice versa)—only a frame. The darker politics which fix that image, or its revision here, to its place do not really enter these pages. (The King assassination occurred perhaps a week after the last incidents I recount; and the horror of Guyana's Jonestown, where the tropic sun was to confound with the human heart of darkness on a scale to silence any Conrad, was inconceivable.) That situation?

It is still Sixty-seven, but we are in New York's Lower East Side. The Northern Hemisphere has begun its annual lean away from the sun. The light is a little colder, harsher, clearer as we enter the autumn and winter following that ebullient summer on another coast . . . .

For a text with even the peculiarly precarious relation to reality of this one to carry the usual fictional disclaimer would be ludicrous. This *is* an essay. But it is not journalism—save in the literal sense that most of the material was first drafted in actual journals kept at the time. In some cases, several persons are combined to make a single character. In others, single persons are atomized to make several. Within the season of our concern, some incidents have been displaced by months; others, by as much as a city. But besides these distortions for essentially musical reasons, every one, thing, and happening is as close as I could make it to *something*. And no character bears a name remotely like any possible model's. In that sense, all that was real, during the winter and spring of '67/'68 on Second Street, was the *Heavenly Breakfast*.

November, 1978
New York

Heavenly Breakfast

An Essay on the
Winter of Love

1

October.
Four rooms on the second floor of a Lower East Side tenement: bathtub in the kitchen; two pantry-sized rooms railroading off that; and a fifteen-by-twenty back room, largest in the apartment.

2

When I walked in, Reema (yes, she had chosen the name herself) kissed me on the neck.

Dave shouted, "Hey, you got here!" and picked me up, arms around my back.

"Please put me down?"

"No. Let me show you around the place."

"Hey—watch it!" I had to hold on to his hair and wrap my legs around his chest to keep from falling. "Put me down!"

"No." He started walking and bumped his hip on the enameled tub cover.

"Look, will you—"

"You tell me where we are." His mouth was muffled on my stomach. "I can't see."

"Then how are you going to—hey!" I ducked. "We just went through a door."

"This is a room."

"Don't step on that—"

"I think I did. That's a laundry bag full of paperback novels under my right moccasin."

"I thought your laundry had corners. *Hey* . . . !" I ducked again.

"This is another room."

"Couldn't you put me down now?"

"No. You'll notice it's painted blue, with white—"

"Left!"

". . . left." A web of leather dragged across my face, brushed against his arms. "That was another door; and this is another room. I don't think there're any more after this one. But I've only been here two months. We sleep in here. Christ, it's good to have you here!"

"It's good to be here." I pulled his right ear.

"Does that mean go right?"

"No," I said. "Where to now?"

"Guide me back to the kitchen."

"Couldn't I walk?"

"I think I ought to carry you awhile. I haven't seen you in a week. You smell."

"Two steps left and forward."

We got back without accident. In the kitchen the bathtub cover was off. Water broke over Reema's feet.

"Is there anything on the kitchen table?"

I looked over my shoulder: "A toaster, a U.S. postal scale, a Martin double-o-eighteen—"

"The toaster isn't on, is it?"

"No."

"Okay. Here you go—"

"Hey!"

2

Dave stood up, face red inside much hair the color of brass shavings.

Reema's knees submerged. "Are you going to stay?" She leaned on the edge and began to sing.

It was a song I'd written.

Then she said: "It would be good to have you . . ." Her hair, like some redder metal, fell over the chipped white.

Sitting on the red-checked oilcloth, I grinned. She began to laugh.

"Yeah. I'm going to stay."

Dave crowed and slapped both hands against the door, and Reema's laughter rose to cross (and momentarily disappeared as it crossed) the sound from the streaming tub tap. (Little Dave, back wedged against the pile of cushions in the corner, looked up from his drawing and grinned. Grendahl, in the stall john in the corner, stood up, zipped his pants, and came out singing the same song. Dominiq, standing on the stool in the middle of the floor, finished replacing the ceiling bulb; it and her smile came on at the same time. Shouldering through the door (as if in answer to Dave's slapping), Joey lugged in a carton of peach (!) wine, the back edge hooked over his turquoise belt buckle—his only flamboyance in otherwise conventional dress: brown slacks, white shirt, sport coat, sneakers . . .

("Chip's gonna stay!"

("Hey, you're really gonna stay?"

("Wow-wee! Have some peach wine!") Reema stood up in the bathtub, fingers, breasts, and knees momentary waterfalls. "Do you want some help bringing your stuff down?" (Anne closed the icebox door, sank teeth into an apple, came by, handed Reema a towel, and went into the back room.

("Wine?" Joey asked.

("Peach?" Reema said. "No thank you."

("I don't need any help," I said, and drank from

3

the proffered bottle—"Thanks . . . that's odd-tasting stuff."

(There were eleven people, all told, in that kitchen.) "Don't you *have* any stuff?" Dave leaned back against the tub and scratched his hair. "Well . . . that just makes it easier, I guess. For a while I didn't know if you would come. I didn't know when."

"With two of the group living here," I said, "it would be a little strange if the other two of us only showed up for rehearsals."

"It could be done. . . ." Dave drank some wine frowned at the bottle, handed it back to Joey (who was saying to Snipper:

"Nobody likes it very much. That's why I bring it around. I can leave half a dozen bottles in somebody's icebox for days, come back, and I know it'll still be there. You want some?")

Dave said: "I didn't set the place here up for the group, you know what I mean?"

I nodded.

"I mean, I set it up to live."

"But," I said, "you've asked us all to live with you. Lee is probably going to be here in a couple of days. So you'll have all four of us here." I looked around at the others.

"I think," Dave said, musing, "that our two weeks' vacation from rehearsals was a very good thing. Maybe it's what we need to get us together. To get it really intense. Now. And here."

"Do you mind," I asked, "if this place here . . . becomes the group?"

"No." Dave swayed forward, then leaned back again, arms folded. "I suppose it would have been perfectly—"

Little Dave tossed him a paisley cushion. He tossed it back.

"—obvious to anyone else. You have a rock group.

4

You have a commune. I guess they're the sort of things that tend to get together."

"You know—" Snipper came up behind Dave's elbow—"you rescued me?"

Dave raised an arm.

Snipper stepped under it. "I was sitting in that furnished room in Brooklyn—" His round glasses flared as he looked up, then cleared from eyelids wrinkled in a grin—"and I played my guitar . . . without any amplifier. You know how little sound a solid-body electric guitar makes with no amplifier? I played that guitar all day long. I hadn't seen anybody in six weeks and . . . yeah, you picked me up and brought me here."

"He does that," Reema said, hair, then head, emerging from ruffled terry cloth.

"Which is my point," Snipper said. "What you want to do—"

"Yeah? What do I want to do . . . ?"

"You want to live with the people around you who make it easier for you to do your work. Which is make music."

"Sure . . ." Dave nodded. "I just wish Lee would get here so we could get started."

3

She arrived the next afternoon, with silver flute, double Indian flute, hose pipe—one end stopped with clay, holes punched down its length for a random scale—panpipes, a transverse flute made of bamboo, about the same length and only slightly thicker than a king-sized beer can; as well as sopranino, soprano, alto, tenor and bass (which Snipper had to stand on a chair to play) recorders; ocarina, kazoo, practice clarinet, nose flute and shawm.

Dominiq pushed the red-and-white-checked table to the side. Grendahl got himself seated on the back of the green overstuffed easy chair. Anne took a walk; and little Dave went into the back room.

In the next two hours, the instrumentation that had been sketched out back in Lee's old apartment where we'd last met was finally set. ("You're really gonna stay here, Lee? You weren't sure for a while . . ."

("Well, the rent ran out on my place two days ago. So I think you're stuck with me." She grinned.) Snipper's line was added to the vocals, and it all nestled down nicely. Dave sang lead:

> *The dawning sky is blue and gray*
> *and blue and gray mists veil the hours,*
> *annul the waters, hide the towers,*
> *erase the spires that crown the bay.*
> *Infinity is blue and gray,*
> *the undefined and incomplete*
> *moment where sky and water meet*
> *before the gray is ripped by day-*
> *blades of gleaming metal gray.*
> *Swimming gull-forms melt and float*
> *in liquid air around the boat*
> *that moans in blind flight on the bay.*
> *A gust of wind throws one more gray-*
> *white bird across the prow. It veers*
> *into the mist and disappears.*
> *In a breath it will be day.*
>
> *Hold me, love; I quake with day,*
> *blind beneath the staring hours.*
> *See the cracked, reflected towers*
> *burning crimson on the bay.*

6

Over Dave, I sang descant—shared once with Lee, sung once alone. Lee and Snipper held fifth and tonic on the last chord, while Dave's voice, then mine, left their suspensions to dive through at the third, his first, major, then mine, minor, to plunge into, and shatter, those reflections.

While Snipper was repatching the amplifiers (and Reema was replaying the test tape, backward), Joey asked: "What's that one called?"

" 'Dawn Passage,'" Snipper said.

"Which one of you guys wrote it?"

I sipped from a jelly jar of hot coffee and raised an acknowledging forefinger. "Music and arrangement."

"And the words."

"Marilyn Hacker."

"No kidding?" Joey said. "Say, why don't you put that stuff down and have some peach wine! That really sounds together."

4

In November 1967 the Second Street apartment became the commune for the now-defunct rock group the Heavenly Breakfast. By the end of the year, both the commune and the group *were* the Heavenly Breakfast. In the decade since, I've met dozens of people who never visited the Breakfast, but either lived in or passed through the Lower East Side that year, and who brought the name up in conversation. It is a small neighborhood with lots of imaginative people:

notoriety spreads quickly. But something about the Breakfast, transmittable even through report, made it, for a while, part of many people's personal mythologies.

This memoir then is basically for myself. Much of what I want to define—for myself—takes back- and high-lights from communal situations I've visited or lived in over the years since. But this first showed me where, among the memories, to search.

I have three notebooks from the period, which from time to time served as diaries. From them and recollection, what can I reconstruct?

The Breakfast was a core of six. Besides Dave, Snipper, Lee and myself—the Heavenly Breakfast rock group *per se*—there was Dave's old lady, Reema; and Grendahl, who just liked to listen to us rehearse, and sometimes played the electric bass. At twenty-one, he had two feet of thick blond hair, already a quarter gray. Also, he was Dave's business partner.

A rock group at the rehearsal stage brings no money in: outlays are heavy. The commune's income came from dealing drugs: grass, hash, acid from the apartment. Speed and scag were in and out as visitors if not supporting members, along with the medicine chest full of acronymic turn-ons: STP, DMT, THC, etc. The drugs were pretty much Dave and Grendahl's department. During the six months I lived there, my personal income was twenty-six dollars: eleven from a story sale, and fifteen from back royalties on a novel. Snipper once got a few bucks for arranging some songs for the Girl Scouts of America. But in the first months, at any rate, those are the only legal incomes I remember among us.

Little Dave, Dominiq, Joey, Anne . . . ? There were another half-dozen people who easily called it home. Distinguishing between them and the core was something I could never have done at the time, and is probably just faulty hindsight on the total length of their residence.

There was, besides, a floating population of twelve to sixteen others, who spent days, weeks, would disappear, then return, spend another day, another week. At least two dozen more always-welcome visitors included a farm commune from New Jersey called Summer, who would drive their twin microbuses into the city for a Fillmore East concert, spend the night afterward rapping with us, smoking dope, drinking wine, maybe falling out for a few hours, a few days.

Not counting perhaps a dozen other tolerated acquaintances, this still made a community of forty-plus. I'd say sixteen was the average number sleeping and eating there any one time.

The bathtub was almost always in use. The stall john in the kitchen had no door. Sex, for all practical purposes, was perpetual, seldom private, and polymorphous if not perverse.

Dave, the oldest mainstay member, was twenty-six. The youngest (floating pop.), excluding parents with todlers/infants, was a Puerto Rican kid named Felix who stayed with us two weeks and told us he was fourteen. He looked younger. I was twenty-five.

In one notebook, I have a list of seventeen initials, ages next to them, totaled and divided: the average age present the evening I made that list was twenty-two.

The kitchen was for visitors, cooking, eating, bathing, rehearsing—

5

This memory interrupts:

Eighteen-year-old Snipper, sitting on the john, head and long hair hung forward, pants down around his sneakers, his long lead-guitarist's fingers limp between small knees. He was constipated and hadn't been able to piss all day. A couple of weeks back he'd had the clap—correction: a couple of weeks back everyone in the Breakfast had had the clap and we'd all gone to the health clinic on Tenth Avenue together (twenty-three, as I recall), but several times since Snipper had wondered aloud if his shots had gotten rid of the infection.

Dave stopped playing his acoustic, uncrossed his legs, and got down from the table. "Hey, man, would it be easier if we all were out of the room?"

Little Dave stopped sketching and looked up. Reema put the cover back on the soup pot and glanced over, licking the spoon.

"I mean," Dave said, "sometimes you just can't get the plumbing to work if a lot of people are sitting around staring at it."

"No . . ." Snipper said. His throat sounded like it was full of sand. "No. Would somebody come and hold my hand, please . . ." Dominiq and I went over and held him.

Half an hour later, when he still couldn't piss, Dave, Dominiq and me put him in a cab and took him to Bellevue in a thin, cold rain.

Later, while we stood around in the yellow-tiled halls, an intern explained that Snipper had apparently had, possibly for several years, a retentive urethral fungus the clap had irritated. The gonorrhea was gone but a secondary infection had set in.

Snipper was very ill.

The intern, brushing at his stained whites, looked at our long hair, our old clothes, and chewed on the inside of his lip: "We had a kid in here a couple of weeks ago with the same thing," he said offhandedly, "who died. Clap, fungus, all that scar tissue in the tubes—same thing. But he lived at home and was scared to tell his folks about any of it. Until it was too late."

Two weeks later, Snipper's plumbing was back in order. Reema, Dominiq, and Lee brought him home from the hospital.

"Man!" he announced from the doorway, glasses flaring. The three women laughed loudly around him. "When they stuck that catheter in me, the other end fell out of the sink and spurted across the whole goddamn room. Just be glad I *didn't* piss while I was here. I had so much juice in me, I would have drowned you!"

<hr>

6

This is how things were decided at the Breakfast:

One afternoon, Little Dave, still half asleep, came out of the back room into the kitchen and said: "Okay . . . I'm gonna mop the floor today. Everybody get out. Go on, get into the back or somewhere. Or take a walk. Yeah, all of you. I want to get this place clean."

"And leave your shoes off when you come back in," Lee added, as she got up to go. She was just a breath under six feet tall—when her hair was pulled back tight in a dull bronze horsetail. "That way we can keep it clean."

"Yeah," Little Dave said. "Everybody just take your shoes off when you come in the door from now on."

Somebody came in the door.

Grendahl put his hand on her shoulder. "From now on when you come in, take your shoes off at the door, okay?"

"Okay," Judy said. "Sure."

Little Dave was already running water in the zinc pail from under the sink.

The shoes-off policy was kept up till the Breakfast disbanded.

We never had anything even resembling an organizational meeting. If you wanted something done, you did it; if you wanted people to do something, you asked them. The goad to do something someone wanted you to do was having to live with that person's discomfort or disapproval if you didn't do it. As close as *we* lived, that was quite a goad.

By this method, the two little rooms were set aside for people who were doing something that required physical solitude: transcribing music from tapes or instruments (Dave couldn't read music), or working on a vocal line with one other person. Or writing music. Later, one of the other rooms became an electronics shop for amplifiers and things when Little Dave set up his repair equipment there. Loose wires? Hot solder? They needed privacy.

The back room was for the dozen-plus people actually sleeping there: you balled, slept, kept your instruments, your other possessions there—clothes, books, a crystal of pink quartz, a set of felt-tipped pens, some miniature houses with trees and lawns, a suburb that could sit on Lee's belly as she regarded it between her breasts.

You didn't go into the back room unless you were sleeping at the Breakfast. If you didn't pick up on that pretty fast, or had to be told more than once, you were not a welcome visitor, but a tolerated acquaintance.

The Heavenly Breakfast was not particularly democratic.

There was nothing terribly collective about it either—though a good deal of clothing was shared. But the bundles by the bed or mattress you were sleeping on that night were yours. What was in your instrument case was left alone.

There was one built-in corner cabinet in the back room, with drawers beneath. "That one," Little Dave said, "is going to be for my drawing stuff."

"Okay if I put my typewriter in there too?" Snipper asked. "There's room on the side." He was writing a novel that week.

"Sure."

Later, Grendahl started keeping his jewelry there. It became the communal drawer for private property.

Because (Big) Dave and Grendahl managed the drug dealing and, therefore, were the only people bringing in money, they paid the rent ($75.00 a month), also paid for food, and if anyone there needed money for something, he asked them for it, got it if they had it, didn't if they didn't.

But neither of them did much cleaning or cooking.

There was an exercise bar across the door from the kitchen to the first little room. Anne, who was a senior at NYU and on the women's tumbling team, and Snipper were taking turns working out, naked, on the bar.

"You know," I said to Dave, who had just looked up

13

from his book where he sat on the corner cushions, "three days ago, when I got here, you know what I was worried about most?"

Anne's feet went between her arms; she released one hand, rotated—Snipper, spotting, kept her from bumping the doorjamb—and recovered, going into a crab-hang, cunt thrust toward us.

"What?"

"Privacy. But I've discovered something, just since I've been here. It's very difficult to be alone in a room with only two or three other people. In a room with fifteen or twenty, though, it's easy. When your facial expression or some body movement hints at the least thought of privacy, there're enough other people to pay attention to so that everyone turns away. And you're alone. Then, as soon as somebody wants to be a part, when his head lifts, or his eyes seek, somebody's there."

"Yeah." Dave grinned. "When you've been here awhile, you almost get too dependent on that." And while I wondered what he meant, he dropped his eyes back to his book.

Anne lifted Snipper to the bar. He swung from side to side to adjust his grip, then turned over and through in a skin-the-cat, reversed, and came back again for a one-legged hang, a thin bag of bone and flesh. But you were more conscious of the bone.

7

We averaged five meals a day.

Reema and Little Dave did most of the day-to-day cooking. Eggs, hash, home fries, pancakes, toast from an eccentric pre-World War II toaster which, were it not watched carefully, would burn four more neat holes in the oilcloth; apple and pear juice; cabbage, squash—zucchini, butternut, and acorn—collards, spaghetti sauce going for hours; chickens, chops, roasts; and lots more pancakes.

There were no official sleeping shifts but more people tended to be awake between noon and midnight than between midnight and noon: five meals worked out pretty well.

Maybe twice a week, when the regular cooking flagged, I'd fix boned ducks stuffed with fruit and sausages, mushroom salad, an array of curries; sometimes just a stew, hush puppies; lemon-chiffon cake; a platter of baked bananas with lemon juice, flamed in brandy.

And while we rehearsed and ate and lounged and cleaned, Dave and Grendahl did about seven hundred dollars a month business in grass to Vassar girls and off-duty cops, servicemen, musicians, our Puerto Rican neighbors, turnouts from mental hospitals, a bunch of photographers who kept coming to do a photo essay on the place for the *Evergreen Review* that never materialized. Considering they supported a dozen-plus people single-handed, it wasn't much.

"Hello!" Grendahl said, coming in. "This is Paul. He's going to buy some dope." Paul came in behind him.

Some people said hello. Those near got introduced.

Paul wore a mustard corduroy suit and grinned a lot. He was big as a tackle, had dark yellow skin and light yellow hair. He was nervous when he entered, and masked it with a perpetual grin. After he relaxed a little he started saying, as a lot of people said, "This is really a great place. Yeah, I really like this." As he wandered around the kitchen, or explored the little rooms, he became more voluble: "How long have you lived in here? I mean, all of you haven't been here for all that time. No, I mean, which ones of you came here first. Oh, you three . . . ? No kidding!" Grendahl was weighing out Paul's grass.

Paul stood by the stove, looking across at Grendahl working with the scales at the table. "You keep a lot of dope around here, don't you? You guys got anything else besides grass? How much do you actually keep here? Do you have it all here, or is some of it stashed other places?" (I was already uncomfortable, but that was the one that stopped me. It didn't stop Paul, though.) "Where do you get this much dope? What do you mean, you don't *know* where you get it. Come *on* . . . Oh, I see! You think I'm going to go buy it from your source." He laughed. "That's a good one! Naw, I wouldn't do that. You guys look like good people. I like you. So I'll buy my dope from you, see?"

Grendahl was pretty affable. Like I said, he was just twenty-one. Paul's whole spiel had left him pretty unperturbed.

They smoked some.

Paul left with three ounces.

When the door closed behind him, I looked up from the vocal arrangement I was plotting out for the next tape rehearsal with Magic Markers on graph paper.

"Hey," Dave said. "You with the hair all down your ass."

Hair swung as Grendahl turned. He was grinning happily as Paul had been when he left.

"Do yourself, do us all a favor. Don't bring him back in here. Really."

Grendahl's grin flattened. "Why?"

Lee, in the corner, regluing the pads on her silver flute, turned around and grunted as though she'd been punched. "What," she demanded, "was that shit about how much grass do we have and where it comes from! Yeah. You better leave him outside."

"I thought he was a nice guy," Grendahl said. "I wouldn't have brought him around if I didn't think he was a nice guy. Sure, he talks too much. But he had money and he wanted some dope."

Dominiq's brown hands came around the doorjamb and she peered in. "I was about to go up the damn wall," she said, "and I was in the other room. Is he a narc or something?"

"He may indeed be a nice guy," Joey said over the mouth of his bottle, "but you will notice I offered him none of my peach wine." He raised his bottle meaningfully and took another swallow.

Grendahl pulled his gray-shot hair over his shoulder and hung on it, which he did whenever he was confused. "You think he was a narc?"

"He could be," Joey said. "And you got busted once already for selling to the wrong people. You know him for a long time?"

"That don't mean nothing," small Felix said (who was there that week), "narcs hang around for months sometimes."

"I met him yesterday," Grendahl said. "He just wanted to cop—shit, I don't want to get involved with *another* fucking narc!"

"Any narc," I said (and Dave, standing behind him, had already put both hands on Grendahl's shoulders),

17

"who was that uncool would've lost his job a long time
back. He isn't a narc. But he likes the place. He wants
to come back. And he isn't very cool. He's not going to
be any problem himself. But he's the kind of guy
that'll bring a friend around someday . . . just to
show him what a great place this is. And his *friend*
will be the narc."

"I won't bring him back then," Grendahl said. "I
guess I just won't bring him back. I've been through
that once. I don't want to go through it again."

That was the closest thing we had to a drug problem.

In rooms full of fine people, it's nice to have three
or four of them always around naked. It's nice to have
a few others dressed in silver, in paisley, in leather, in
fur, in something pastel and transparent that sways, in
something brocade or velvet that swings; people on
their way to a concert, a big deal, a little deal, a
friend, or just going for (or returning from) a walk.
And it's nice to have most of the people knocking
around in something once beautiful, with wear grown
comfortable.

8

There were two big mattresses in the back room that
could each hold four easily, and four smaller ones that
could each hold two or three. In a communal situation
bisexuality has to be of at least passing interest to
everyone. (That's assuming both sexes are repre-
sented.) The standard bohemian/liberal education

teaches you quickly not to take offense at someone else's desire. If it pleases you, you move toward it; if not, you sidestep politely as your individual temperament allows. At the Breakfast I learned to move within the circle of other people's desire, and be at ease as I generated my own. And I would strike one of my senses before I would part with that knowledge.

Some twelve of the eighteen there had dropped acid that evening. The windows were aglitter with slush and the sashes crashed in their frames from the wind. Lee and I lay on one of the small mattresses in the back. We hadn't taken any because we'd been involved in a very intense and quiet conversation that had begun with some new ideas about song arrangements and had now moved on to gossip about some friends outside the Breakfast.

Snipper had dropped a tab and a half and all his clothes; for the last hour he'd been standing on a pile of blankets in the corner playing, on a nylon-string guitar, a song about a bicycle race during which a lot of people got married and several railway trains arrived and departed.

Now he put down his instrument, came to our bed, crawled between Lee and me, and lay on his stomach, face on his folded arms, hips wedged between our groins. We went on talking over his shoulder blades.

Reema walked in, picked up Snipper's guitar, glanced at us, went into another room, and began to play, clumsily, at the bicycle song.

While I went on talking, I began to rub Snipper's back. Finally he turned over, grinning. He had a hard-on.

"Which one of us is responsible for that?" Lee asked.

Snipper lifted his head, looked down at himself, then back and forth between Lee and me, shrugged, lay back down and said, "How should I know?"

Eyes wide, he touched our faces.

I rubbed his chest, his groin.

Lee began to rub his belly.

We all made out together for a while, in the middle of which Grendahl came in and said to Joey and Dominiq, who were reading on the other side of the room, and to Little Dave, who was sketching on the mattress next to us, "I just made a very large salad if anyone wants some."

"I am enjoying this," Snipper said from somewhere underneath, "but I am also much too high to come. And I would like to see something green—if not a tree, a piece of lettuce."

"I," whispered Lee, "am awfully hungry."

"Let us," I said, "get up, then, and go into the kitchen." Which, that time, is what we did.

If you've ever indulged the fantasy of being invisible, you'd probably like commune life. It allows you to enjoy the part of the fantasy that's healthy play, and forces you to terms with the part that's neurotic escape—if you want to keep playing. Not everyone, though, who would like such a life can actually live it.

9

One person's fantasy is another's reality. The difference between fantasy and the real, however, is that the ethical and moral implications the fantasy has for the person who indulges it are always ones brought to it from a prior reality. The ethical and moral implications for those who live through what might once have been for them a fantasy situation *can* come from the reality of that situation; and so may be very different.

One evening, there was a knock. While two people moved out of the way so that Dave, loping up from the corner cushions, could open the door—he was expecting someone—it swung back before he reached it, and a head with blond hair all around it pushed through, leering quizzically. "Hello? Is anybody home . . . ?"

"Yeah?" Dave said. More would have been superfluous. There were eight people there.

The door opened all the way. The stocky man stepped in. He wore a green service coat over a wool shirt, with butter-colored hair tufting between the top buttons.

From Dave's expression, I could tell it wasn't whom he'd been expecting.

"Oh, hi, Bob," Dominiq said, coming into the room. "I wasn't sure whether that was your voice."

"Hi!" Bob said. His voice was quiet, low, and pleasantly rough. "I thought I'd come up and see what kind of place you guys had here. You made it sound pretty interesting when I met you on the street last week, all muffled up in your army jackets." He shrugged his off and put it on a chair. "So I thought I'd check it out."

"Yeah," Dave said. "Sure."

Bob said, "What's in here?" and brushed by Dominiq to go into the darkened little room, where somebody coming from the back said, "Excuse me . . . ?"

Bob's voice returned from the darkness: "I was just looking around your place. So far, it looks . . . um—" tentative now, as I pictured him face to face with Lee in the inner doorway—". . . pretty nice. I mean, I just wanted to look around."

"Go on," I heard Lee say. "Only we don't have visitors in the back unless they're sleeping here."

"Oh," Bob said. "I'm sorry. I'll—"

"No. You go on. Look."

". . . well, thanks."

A couple of us exchanged glances.

A shy minute later, Bob, having looked, returned to the kitchen. He was still smiling. "Got a really nice place here. There were some people asleep back there, but I don't think I woke them up. . . . Really feels nice. I could enjoy living in a place like this. It feels nice all over." Then he sat down on the edge of the tub, where Little Dave was taking a bath, and started talking with Reema and me, who were cooking.

The person Dave was expecting arrived.

A lucrative grass deal for two ki's made everyone feel better. We all got high. Reema invited Bob to stay for dinner. Bob asked if there was enough—there was plenty—and went downstairs and returned with five large bottles of black-cherry soda.

After we finished the chicken and black-eyed peas (and cherry soda), Snipper brought out his box of colored Pentels and Little Dave contributed some paper. Bob wrote out all our names in twenty-three different lettering styles, from stark to ornately, beautifully, and illegibly complicated (he said he was trying to match our personalities to the lettering, and took samplings of our own handwriting to help him), rapping down the history of each. He was a free-lance calligrapher and had worked for several design houses. It was a good evening.

The next time Bob visited, he carried a canvas shoulder bag of inks, lettering pens, lettering brushes, and various samples of papers, parchments, and vela. While we watched, he invented three Heavenly Breakfast lettering styles. Cross-legged on the floor cushions, using the first BeeGees' album for a backboard, he wrote out Snipper's: "The Heavenly Breakfast is the people living together who make working together easier," in New York *Times* Gothic; Anne tacked it over the door for a motto. "Are you sure you know what we're doing here?"—Dave's most frequent phrase in rehearsals—came out in a style Bob christened "Babel-17." That was Scotch-taped to the flaking green wall of the john above the toilet-paper roller held on by one screw. Reema's "Somebody look at the toaster," in balloonlike pastels, went up over the kitchen table beside a portrait of Lee in the World's Most Surrealistic Bathtub—a host of creatures in the steam, with Rube Goldberg water fixtures and drain-pipes—that Little Dave had done one day when he was high and Lee had been taking a bath.

From the first, Bob was fond of us.

He came by often, often saying how much he'd like to live there.

We were fond of him.

Dave and I were coming back to the Breakfast one evening. It had been snowing for half an hour; but already, at fire hydrants, garbage cans, and before bottom stoop steps, the blue-white veil had bruised to slush. As we passed through the furious glitter beneath the streetlamp on Avenue C and Fifth, I asked: "What is it about Bob? He's a little pushy, sometimes; but he's nowhere near as loud as Grendahl. What's the reason none of us want him to move in?"

"He wouldn't like living there." When it's actually snowing in New York, it isn't that cold. The flurry had caught Dave in just a flannel shirt: he was walking tall, ignoring the flakes powdering his hair and shoulders. He pushed his hands down into his green fatigue pants pockets, considering his own pronouncement.

When we reached the far curb, I said: "Yeah, I guess I have that feeling too. But I wonder why. . . ."

And a few nights later, this:

Lots of the Breakfast had gone to a concert at the Yiddish Anderson. Others were out in New Jersey at Summer, helping to finish building a house in the

snow. There were only five of us there that evening
when Bob knocked.

Anne had taken off her clothes and was sitting on
the corner cushions smoking a cigarette, a copy of an
Updike novel, spine down, on one kneecap.

At the kitchen table—we'd both stripped to jeans—
Lee and I were copying out lead sheets: Snipper, who
had managed to lose his recently completed novel,
was making up for it with a very prolific week of
songwriting.

The radiators hadn't turned off yet. As in many
Lower East Side apartments, when there was heat at
all, there was too much.

Bob shed his coat, wandered around, finally unbuttoned his shirt and pulled it out of his belt, but didn't
take it off. Once, I think, he looked in the icebox,
once peered in the back room—("Is that Dominiq and
Grendahl asleep in there?"

("I think so," I said. "I'm not sure.")—sat down in
the green chair to read a book, but got up after a few
pages, lifted up a pot lid from a kettle on the back of
the stove—

"If you're hungry, rinse out a bowl," I suggested.

"Naw," he said.

I told him, "Help yourself if you change your
mind."

—and went and looked at the Indian print Judy had
hung across the wall the day before.

"I think," Lee said, balancing her chair on the back
legs, with upraised arms and swiveling fists, "I'm
going to take a break." The forelegs tapped down. She
walked over to Anne, who said:

"I'm not going to read the last six pages of this." She
patted the cushion beside her. "Come on. Sit here."

Lee sat. The two of them started talking.

"Does anyone want some tea?" Bob asked.

The song I was notating changed time signatures
one measure before the break. I debated whether to

transcribe it informally with a fermata, or write it all out. It was called *Alembic*.

Lee and Anne were laughing about something.

"Is it all right if I make some tea?"

One of us nodded.

After a while Bob said: "It's ready. Does anyone want some tea besides me?"

"Okay," Anne said. "I'll have some." She was sitting behind Lee, now rubbing Lee's shoulders because Lee said she'd been bent over the goddamned lead sheets so long her back was sore. (She had been working about four hours longer than I had.) Lee's head was forward and her hair hung straight to the lap of her jeans. Anne had very strong hands—from her tumbling. When she kneaded the small, knobby bones of Lee's collar, the blond column of Lee's hair swayed.

Bob brought cups for them both.

Lee leaned back against Anne, her hair divided in four by her face and breasts.

Then Bob brought his own cup over to them and sat on the floor, sipping. Neither of the women drank any of theirs. But all three of them talked awhile. Anne kept massaging Lee's neck.

I looked around for a new piece of music paper and found one that had slipped down between the wall and the back table leg.

I heard Bob say to the bottom of his empty teacup, "Well, maybe I should be on my way."

"You don't have to." Anne reached to rub Bob's neck under his yellow beard. "Your neck feels very different from Lee's."

"It ought to," Bob said, still into his cup. "I'm ten years older than you two."

"It feels nice," Anne said, "too."

Lee went into the back room first. Anne picked up the Updike again, read another half-page, said: "I'm *really* not going to finish this," stood up, and went inside.

Bob got up, went to the stove, started to pour himself another cup, didn't, came over to me, and whispered: "Should I go back there?"

At least five times during their conversation, Bob had said: "I've thought a lot about going to bed with two women at once." Anne had said it sounded like "fun" and Lee said it at least sounded "interesting."

"Sure," I said. "If you want."

Bob went to the doorway and took a breath. (I remembered how he'd barged through it on his first visit.) He walked, carefully, forward.

I decided to notate *Alembic* in a new time signature after all.

Five minutes later, Bob came out, shirt in one hand, his sneakers in the other. His jeans were unbuttoned at the waist but the fly was zipped.

He grinned, a little halfheartedly. "I guess I'll be on my way," he whispered, put his sneakers on the floor and leaned back against the table corner to pull on one bright red sock.

"Change your mind?"

He shrugged. "Well, you know . . . They were doing things. With each other. . . . I mean, even after I got into it . . . too. And that . . ." He shrugged again.

I raised an eyebrow, then shrugged back.

Bob left.

Ten minutes later, people got back from Summer. The kitchen was pretty busy for a while. But I was tired. So I went in the back room.

The radiator ceased hissing.

Lee and I usually slept in the bed by the back window. She was a rumple of hair and blue blankets, grayed from the trapezoid of light on the flaked ceiling.

I sat down on the bed to pull my jeans off. She turned over to curl around me, knees against my hips. "Hi," she said. "You finished?"

"Nope," I said. "Just tired," and got into bed as she uncurled. "Wanna ball?"

She nodded into my neck.

Dave and Reema came inside and began shedding clothes against the checkered light through the leather webbing that hung across the door.

Dave sat down on a bed and I heard him whisper: "Hey, who're you?" He sounded tired.

"Me," Anne answered sleepily.

"Oh," Dave said. A triangle of darkness from the raised blanket; then the blanket fell. "Move over a little, huh?"

Somebody else said, "Sure."

The beds squeaked and rustled.

I reached across Lee's shoulder to the windowsill where she kept her foam—she was on a six-month break from the pill—and she said, "That's all right. I put some in when Bob was here." The expression I could feel against my shoulder, rather than see, was a frown. "He's very strange. I'm glad he's not living here."

"Me too."

Dave and Reema were making it.

Balling someone you've been working hard with, for me at any rate, is one of the most satisfying things I know. It was a good night.

10

Bob came around maybe two times a week now instead of four.

And he stopped saying he wanted to move in.

Was he more relaxed during the times he visited? Or did having him around a little less make us more friendly during the time he was there, which he reflected? Either one, or in combination, I suspect some element of his fantasy had died. But when he came around to dinner, he still brought soda, and sometimes beer. And he volunteered to letter our first album, whenever we got one, which we all thought was a fine idea.

11

One day near the end of November, I took a walk after rehearsal. When I came home, I found Little Dave had brought two friends who were going to stay with us awhile: Liz and her two-year-old son, Electric Baby. I guess I got points for not asking why she named her son Electric Baby. In twenty minutes, though, I was calling him Electro—I think somebody else started it—only to discover that to Liz, his mother, he was simply "E." I do recall, once, Grendahl asking: "What's his name going to be when he's fourteen or fifteen? Electric Adolescent?" But I don't think that was when Liz was in the room.

When Little Dave said that dinner was ready, Liz surprised us by saying she and Electric Baby would skip eating with us that night. She was on a macrobiotic diet and she would cook up some brown rice later. Electro was asleep on the green easy chair, one fist off the cushion, the other under his chin.

He didn't wake up until the rest of us had nearly finished. When he did, though, he sat up, slid down to the floor, walked up to Snipper, who was sitting at the table, and said, "I'm hungry. Can I have something to eat?"

Snipper paused with a forkful of pork, looked at Liz: ". . . Is it all right if I give him something now?"

Liz, sitting on the covered bathtub, reading, glanced up. "No. He can't have any of that kind of food. Come on, E. It's not good for you. Now, don't bother people."

Electro turned around and came over to the stove, where I was helping myself to more gravy. "Can you give me something to eat?"

"Your mom says you have to wait."

"I'm hungry. . . ?" He looked up at the bottom of the plate—a pie pan, actually—I was using.

"I don't know what to tell you," I said.

Liz had gone back to her book.

Electro put his hands over the bib of his blue corduroys and went over to Lee, who was sitting on the floor by the bookshelf. "Can I have something to eat? I'm hungry."

"Your mom says . . . well, you heard." Lee frowned toward Liz, then back at Electric Baby. He was a very blond and, right now, a very dirty baby.

Barefoot and shirtless, he had a bony little chest and a funny sort of panting way of breathing.

Electro walked over to Dave, who didn't wait to be asked; he put his hand on the back of Electro's neck and called over to Liz: "When did you guys eat last, anyway?"

"Last night—well, late last night, I think. But that's because it's so hard to really be strict about cooking. Especially when you're doing it at other people's houses." She closed the book with her thumb in the place. "But I'm never very hungry anyway."

"I think," Dave said, rubbing Electro's back, "you better start fixing some food."

"In a little while." Liz smiled and opened up her book.

About ten minutes later, she put on a pot of brown rice to boil.

Half an hour later (brown rice takes about forty-five minutes to cook) Lee was passing the stove, looked in the pot, and asked, "That's for you *and* Electro there . . . ?"

"Well," Liz said, "we don't need very much."

They ate, Liz at the table, Electro on the floor beside her; he finished his rice in thirty-four seconds flat. Then he stood up in front of his mother and asked: "Can I have some of yours?"

"Now we have to share things," she told him. But she gave him another spoonful.

With the spoon in his mouth, handle in both hands, Electro ambled across to the green easy chair and leaned against it, sucking.

On the stove was a tray with six porkchops left from dinner; among them, a dozen broiled mushrooms glistened with juice. The tray was partly on one burner, so that one corner was clear of gravy, and the heavier drippings had browned at the edge and curled.

What did it for me was when Liz, walking to the

sink to leave her plate, passed the stove, picked up a chop with two fingers, dunked it in the thinner gravy and took a bite.

We never discussed what happened next. But the following things did, practically at the same time:

From across the room, I said: "Hey, I bet that's not on your macrobiotic diet."

Liz turned around, surprised.

I grinned: "But it tastes good, doesn't it?"

Liz smiled, a bit embarrassed, and walked a couple of steps from the stove. "Sometimes I slip up and nibble. But really, this kind of food, meat and stuff, is so awful for you. Of course I'm more concerned about E than I am about myself."

I nodded.

Meanwhile:

As soon as mom had picked up the chop, Electric Baby had put down his spoon on the chair cushion and beelined for the stove.

Grendahl, who was standing by the oven, as soon as Liz turned to answer me, picked up another chop and held it down near the torn knee of his jeans—at about two-and-a-half-year-old eye level.

Electric Baby swerved, and got it with fingers and teeth at once.

Grendahl jerked his hand away, shook his head, then patted the back of E's head, who went, gnawing contentedly, back to the chair.

And meanwhile:

Everybody else there decided that the next time Electric Baby said he was hungry, we'd feed him.

"I used to cook macrobiotic," I said to Liz. "For nearly a year."

"You did?" She looked surprised. "Why did you stop?"

"I go back to it occasionally to sort of clean out the system. But you can't do it really strictly in this climate or geographic area."

Lee came up to listen, taking another mushroom en route. "I've had some really great macrobiotic meals." (She stood more or less in the line of sight between Liz and the chair.)

"To make it work, you've got to eat all the vegetables that grow in your own area: carrots, wheat, cabbage, tomatoes—"

"Aren't tomatoes too yang?" Liz asked.

"Yin," I said. "But if you've been eating nothing but brown rice, which, after it ages, tends to go yang, you've got to balance it off with *some*thing."

At this point Liz saw Electric Baby with his porkchop but she was still cornered by the conversation. Frowning past us, she asked: "What about . . . mushrooms? *They* must be good for you."

While Lee took another bite, I said, "No food value at all—in ordinary nutritional terms. But they have trace amounts of zinc and manganese, without which you get sick and die young."

Liz sort of stuck to her diet. Basically, she was a young woman who didn't like to eat. But from then on, we fed Electric Baby, and as long as somebody talked to her about it, she didn't seem to mind. Two weeks later, when they left, he looked a lot healthier.

There was food there; we fed him. And that first time was the only time we did it all secretively.

12

Snipper, Judy, and I were coming across garbage-strewn Second Street when we were stopped by a man in a tweed sports jacket with a clipboard. He had on a scarf and knitted gloves, and his pale breath kept drifting in front of his very pink face. It had been much warmer that morning. "Excuse me, do you have a minute to take part in an opinion poll?"

"About what?" I asked.

"The war in Vietnam."

"I don't think I'm interested."

"Wouldn't you like to register your opinion?"

"No."

"I mean, it's not going to be used against you. You don't have to sign anything."

I said, "If I did, I'd be more willing . . . but not willing enough."

"You people down here . . ." He looked around at the street. (In duffel coats, a long-haired couple was turning the corner.) "You aren't very cooperative. I'm just doing my work. I get paid for this . . ." I think it dawned on him how banal he sounded, because he laughed a little. "I don't go around in a tie *all* the time." Well, his hair was short. "The political indifference down here, I don't think it's a very good sign."

"It's a bad sign," Judy said. "We're not indifferent. That's why we don't want to help with your survey."

"You're not being very cooperative," he repeated.

"On your form," I asked, "does it have a place to

put down the number of people who refuse to cooperate?"

"No," he said and put his head to the side. "We don't."

"Then it isn't any use to me."

He pulled his clipboard tighter in against his stomach. "I don't think I appreciate this attitude you people have down here," he repeated.

We walked away.

In my notebook, when I finished jotting down the above incident, sitting on the back-room windowsill at the Breakfast, I made this entry:

"All political action within a given political system perpetuates that system if only because that system has defined which actions are and which actions are not political. But when all questions of politics, from policy to the presidential election, follow the semantic form 'Have you stopped beating your wife?' the spectrum from *yes* through *maybe* to *no* is a meaningless range of answers.

"The purpose of following the above anecdote about the interviewer in the street with the above statement is to remind myself that while both are true, they have nothing to do with each other.

"I am as sure that the young man with his clipboard is opposed to the war as he, no doubt, is sure that we are. Our differences are purely personal, as are all political encounters within the statistical matrix of a megalithic republic. How terrible that we were forced to stand there, degrading one another's intelligence, insulting each other's integrity, and generally indulging in such civil barbarousness."

13

A couple of days after Liz and Electric Baby left, another friend of Little Dave, named Janice, dropped by for the afternoon. This from somewhere in the conversation: "Liz . . . ? Yes, she stayed with Billy and me for three days, once. I guess that was just before she came here. It was just awful. Because we couldn't do anything about feeding her kid, short of outwardly defying her. It's pretty hard to get between a mother and child tactfully. My two were eating away, and having to say no whenever E would ask—I hated it. We just didn't know what to do. I'll never know how you guys did it."

The only suggestion I could offer is that somehow, because of the number of us living so closely at the Breakfast, there were enough people in the commune to take care of Liz and Electric Baby at the same time, whereas there hadn't been with just Janice and her folk. I doubt if our effect was permanent—shortly I heard that Liz and Electric Baby had taken off for the West Coast. We probably came closer than anyone else, though.

14

We'd had two snows, and a freezing week; then the last of autumn reasserted itself. For three days it was warm enough outside in the street for shirt sleeves. (Only on the second one, though, did they turn off the heat inside the apartments.)

By the rustle of the bedding about me and the shaking of the mattress beneath, I heard/felt Lee sit up. She shook my shoulder: "Come on. Time to move."

"Why?" I inquired of the inside of my elbow.

"Because," Lee said, "I want to go out now, and you told me to wake you up when I did. And I have."

"Oh." I went about tensing this muscle, then that one, to see if, on relaxing, blood would fill them. Then I opened my eyes.

Lee was butting through the collar of her blue sweatshirt. "Are you going to come visiting with me today?"

"Now remind me what we're supposed to be doing," I said.

"You remember, I told you I met Eddy and Linda and that spade kid—Gerry, I think his name was?"

I grunted.

"They have a sort of commune on the dead-end street—"

"Fifth?"

"Yeah. They said we should drop over. I wanted to see what kind of place they had."

All of which began to come back to me. So I stretched and punched around in the shadow-filled room, putting on pants, sneakers—"You got a shirt anywhere around?"

"Here's a vest," Lee said. "It's still warm out."—and vest. Then we went outside, where it wasn't *that* warm. But the sky was clear and you could still see all the way to the river down the side streets.

15

The alley behind the schoolyard: beer cans flattened with the indent of an instep, one twisted (aluminum cans with concave bottoms were only a few months old) to a flaky rope, others just bent. D T K L M F , sprayed across the brick with an aerosol can of purple paint, lingered from when I'd lived on this block four years ago.

I said: "I used to live on this block four years ago."

A brown bag had been walked to mush on one side; and where the wire fence, bound to rusty pipes, hit the paste of soot and water, a little dirty grass still grew.

"It must be a lot worse since then." Lee put her hands in her back pockets.

"Better, actually."

She wrinkled her nose as we came around the corner onto the street.

"In here?" I asked.

"Yeah."

I glanced at the boarded windows, then followed

her down the steps. "There used to be a doctor's office in here four years ago. Do we just knock . . . ?"

In the vestibule was a side door. "Just go in, they said." She pushed at the door. "Their lights got turned out about a month or so back and no one's had the bread to get them turned on again." About a foot in, the door hit something soft: someone behind it grunted.

I looked down.

A naked leg bent at the knee. A shoulder under a lot of hair came forward, about level with my thigh.

"Visitors . . ." Lee called out, not loudly.

The door had been stopped by a mattress.

"You want us to come back later?" Lee asked.

"Naw." He pushed hair from face and, squatting, naked, on the balls of bare feet, held the edge of the door with one hand. "Come in. Come on in, if you want."

Lee looked at me. So I edged in—sneaker onto blankets, first step; and gritty floorboards, the second. Flakes of light came through the boarded-up window to litter the table, on the corner of which—the only neat thing I saw—was a stack of three-inch yellow manila envelopes.

The table edge was a comb of cigarette burns. Somewhere I could smell candle wax; I didn't see any candles burning, though.

"Don't close the door," the naked guy on the mattress said to Lee after she was in. "It's the only light we get in here." He pulled up the foot of the mattress, which let the door open all the way, then wedged the door edge against the mattress's doubled side.

A flat of light crossed the strewn floor and lit a wall all shaling plaster and blue peelings.

The guy stood up, one arm, one hip, half his hair and one bony knee illuminated, while he pulled on some jeans, stepping about for balance.

Another person on another mattress turned over and rubbed her eyes.

Another voice said, "What you doing down there?" and we heard movements from some loft construction in the back.

Since the time I'd been in it as a doctor's office, the waiting room had been made into one apartment; the examination rooms, presumably, were now another, with a different entrance farther down the hall.

"Watch out, man. I'm coming over," the other voice continued.

"I'm watching," a woman's grunted back.

The guy who'd let us in said, "Who'd you come to visit?"

"Eddy . . . ?" Lee offered.

The guy said into the darkness, "Is Eddy here?"

"Yeah, I'm here. I'm coming out in a minute. . . . Hey, watch out, man!"

"I'm watching! I'm watching!" And a tall black guy with dozens of little braids all over his head like charred matches ambled forward. He wore a pair of khaki pants torn off short and sandals that had as much brass—buckles, chain, and ornamental plate—as leather. "Hello." He smiled over a missing tooth. "I think Eddy's coming now. I'm Gerry."

"Yeah. I'm coming—oh, hey! It's you! Hello!"

"Hello," Lee said into the dark, while I shook Gerry's hand.

A thin girl, canary blond, wearing a white wrinkled smock, wandered unsteadily forward.

Gerry's pink-palmed hand went from mine to take her shoulder; he guided her against him. She settled under his arm, face to his chest. A delicate, grubby fist with pink, bitten nails relaxed near her white-lashed eyes. The pink toes of one foot forked the smudged heel of the other. Gerry dropped his chin to inquire: "How you feeling today, Lady? You feel better?"

She gave small nod and made small moan.

"Lady had a miscarriage yesterday," Gerry explained. "Yesterday, we were up at the hospital all morning." He dropped his chin again. "Lady, you should *tell* somebody when you're gonna have a baby."

"I did," Lady said. "When I first met you in the park, two days ago, I told you."

"Told some *other* people," Gerry said, "and a long time ago. Well, you didn't look too well back in the park. Then, yesterday morning, when you started all that bleeding business here! I'll tell you, that was something!"

"If you had a miscarriage yesterday," Lee said, "shouldn't you be in the hospital for a couple of days, just to sort of look out for you?"

"Damn right, she should," Gerry said. "But if you come into the emergency room halfway through a miscarriage, unless you have your own doctor, they just assume you've come from having an unsuccessful abortion—which they don't like. So it's scrape-rape and get on out of here and call us if you start hemorrhaging and can't stop it with a Tampax. They don't want to be involved."

"When are they gonna make abortions legal anyway?" someone said.

"Hi, Eddy," said Lee.

Eddy stepped over a pile of blankets which suddenly sat up and was a young woman already wearing thick wire-framed glasses. "Where's Coca-Cola?" she demanded.

Coca-Cola had to be the guy that had let us in, since he was the only one not there now.

"He just went out," Gerry said. "You have to ask?"

"Oh . . ." Then she blinked at us and smiled. "Hello. I'm Maxine. How are you?" and then began to extricate herself from the olive-drab mound.

"Oh, hey! You came!" Eddy took Lee by both shoul-

ders and squeezed. "That's really great!" He had lots
of black hair that stuck out all over, and pimples.
"And this is . . . ?"

"Chip," Lee said.

Eddy's hands locked my upper arms.

I grinned.

"They're from the Heavenly Breakfast," Eddy explained to Gerry and Lady. "You know, down on Second Street?"

"Yeah. I heard of that," Gerry said. "Glad you could
come around to the Place. It ain't much, though."

(I had to hear "Place" three times before I caught it
as a proper noun.)

"Come on outside!" Eddy led us out to the stoop,
where he sat on the stone siding. He leaned forward
on his thighs. "I'm glad we have a little more sun." He
squinted at the sky. "It's good for my back," which
was as pimpley as his face. "You know—" he hung his
fist in the hammock of his palm between the torn
black denim knees—"I'm really glad you come
around." His bare heels swung against the concrete.
"Hey! Somebody's coming around with a truck in a
little bit. We're all gonna go out to the country. Take
advantage of some of this warm winter weather. You
guys want to come?"

I looked at Lee, whose eyes widened in approval.
"Sure," I said.

"Bring some of your other folks too," Eddy suggested. "As many as can fit. There'll be room. There's
only seven of us."

"Maybe we could take the group," Lee said, "and
rehearse out there?"

"Now, that would really be fine!" Eddy sat up.
"That would be fine!"

The guy who'd let us in, still shirtless and shoeless,
came back down the block, a six-pack of Coca-Cola
clinking at each knee.

Maxine, who, besides her glasses, now wore cowboy

boots, jeans, and a beaded vest, went running toward him. "Darling, you're back! I didn't think I was going to *make* it." She pulled out a bottle, twisted off the cap, and drank deeply. "*Heav*en!" she exclaimed at the end of the swallow. "Now I can face the world!"

"Get your morning caffeine fix!" Coca-Cola bawled out, setting the cartons on the stoop beside Eddy. "Right this way! Caffeine fix, right here! . . . You guys want a Coke?"

Lee took one; so did I.

"Naw," Eddy said. "I don't drink that stuff. It's bad for my skin." Some of the others came out now, got bottles, and settled down to talk.

We asked how long they'd lived there.

Eddy had moved in three months ago. "But I wish the lights and gas were still on. That would make the Place a lot nicer."

Eddy had taken it over when the last people had moved out and left the apartment open. "Left it to me," he explained. "But I like having people around. Lots a friends—sometimes."

Nobody was particularly planning to stay. "But the Place is here if you need it."

Gerry said: "I bet Lady is pretty glad we were here."

From her seat on the steps she gave a small nod, squinting in the morning sun, hands wrapped around the misted, sweating bottle.

I had been expecting a pickup with a psychedelic paint job: a snub-nosed G-M-C diesel came trundling down the street. The cab looked like the first ten feet of a bus sawed loose. The van wasn't too large—a side door on it flapped and clanked as the driver halted and began to back up for the turn, double wheels tilting him suddenly on the curb. Still, it must have been triple the floor area of the Place.

"Hey!" Eddy stood up and shouted back inside. "Riley's here!"

"That's your truck?" Lee asked.

The cab door swung open and a crew-cut blond, with forearms that filled the rolled sleeves of a blue workman's shirt (*Riley* stitched in yellow across the pocket) otherwise a size and a half too big, jumped down on big scuffed construction shoes.

"Hey, Riley; this is Lee, this is Chip, from the Heavenly Breakfast. You remember somebody talking about their place last week? Some of them are going up with us."

Grinning and bobbing, Riley stuck out a hand the size of a small Westphalian ham, every line around nails and knuckles wedged with black grease. His blue pants were bunched, and bunched again at the waist under a beaded Indian belt—the only thing he wore even vaguely 'hip.' Perhaps twenty-three, he was about four feet, ten inches tall.

After we shook, he turned toward the stoop: "Coca-Cola?"

"Yeah?"

"You got one of those for me?"

"Oh, sure, man! Sure, I'm sorry. Here you *go*! Right here!"

Riley leaned his shoulder against the door sill of the cab and drank his Coke, free hand thrust into his pocket, the thumb, with its dirty acorn of a knuckle, outside.

"We gonna put the lock on the door?" Eddy asked.

"You leaving anything inside you don't particularly want stolen?" Gerry asked.

"Hah!" Eddy said and walked away.

"Darling," Maxine said, catching one arm around Eddy's naked shoulders and one arm around Coca-Cola's, "I think it's charming of you two to run around in the altogether like that, just for me, but it *is* December, and though it's warm now, it *may* turn chilly. Especially up where we're going, in the evening."

"I'm taking shoes and stuff," Eddy said, shrugging

away. (It ended up he didn't.) "Coke, you got anything to wear?"

"My pants," Coca-Cola said. "And I got them on."

Behind thick lenses, Maxine's eyes rolled up. "Look, I have that other sweater. So why don't *you* wear it . . ." She ran back into the house.

Riley, still leaning against the truck, tapped the bottom of his empty bottle against the tire, and smiled, and watched. It was easy to see him as an observer from a different world because of his dress and manner; also, because his restrained but intense enjoyment of the rest of them, though engaging, seemed an outsider's still.

The sweater Maxine brought out was gray; when Coca-Cola slipped it on, it turned out to have a tear right under the neck.

"*Fetching!*" Maxine declared. "It's absolutely *you!*"

We climbed into the van.

"Tie that rope to the hook inside so the door don't flop," Riley called back, one foot on the first pipe-step by the cab door.

"Sure thing," Gerry called back. "Lady, you sure you up to the trip? Jimmy's staying back at the Place, so there'll be someone around—"

"I want to go."

"Okay."

I was standing in the van door. Outside, I could see Eddy explaining to Riley, one hand on Riley's dark-blue shoulder: "The Heavenly Breakfast's on Second Street. We'll stop by there first. That's just down there, but you gotta turn the truck around to get out of the dead end."

Riley gave him the biggest grin I could imagine on that small, bony face and said, "I know," in a voice absolutely without emotion. He handed Eddy the empty, climbed into the cab, then shouted down—the goodwill all returned to his voice—"Now, get your pockmarked ass up here, sweetheart! We want to get there *today!*"

Envisaging microbuses and home-built campers, I'd had fleeting concerns whether or not we'd all fit. The van, however, its metal floor covered with plank skids, its corrugated walls hung with green quilt padding, and smelling like a cross between a barn and a print shop, could have held twice the twenty-odd people and their instruments that finally piled into it.

"Christ, this is a big mother!" Dave said, handing me up his guitar case.

We had to make a couple of trips upstairs at the Breakfast to get instruments down. Snipper, Reema, Joey, and a half-dozen others climbed into the back. Somehow when we got going again, Dave and I ended up in the cab with Riley and Eddy.

You know those wire-mesh car cushions you use for summer driving? Riley, to see, had to sit on two, with the backs folded down (which put him maybe a Bronx and a Brooklyn phone directory higher). "Where'd you *get* this truck?" Dave asked over the roaring motor.

Riley just grinned at Dave, pulled at one of the two gearshift knobs and tugged the wheel around. Air blew chilly through the window.

"Riley's my real buddy here," Eddy explained. His arms were out along the seat back. "He picked me up once when I was hitchhiking near Pittsburgh. I told him about New York, about the Place. I don't even think I gave you the address, did I? I just said it was on the dead-end part of Fifth Street. Then I got out and didn't give him another thought. And damned if this half-pint motherfucker didn't haul his thing, clanking and puffing, right on down the block two weeks later."

"You're part of the family, then?" I asked Riley.

"A-number-one," Eddy answered, clapping Riley's far shoulder. He let his hand stay there. "Riley stays with us about half the time and spends the other half over by the docks where he parks the truck sometimes."

"One of you guys get tired," Riley said, "you can crawl up in the sleeper, up back of the seat. It's a little cramped for some people, but it about fits me perfect."

The truck jogged and roared.

The sleeper curtain swung and tickled our shoulders.

"You're from Pennsylvania, huh?" Dave asked. "How long are you planning to stay?"

Riley pulled the wheel around the other way and grinned across Eddy. "Till they catch me." Which Dave apparently thought better not to question.

"You've got a nice setup at the Breakfast." (Eddy had gone upstairs a couple of times to help carry instruments.) "We hear about you a lot. I'm glad we finally got to meet you. It would be nice if we had the Place like that. I mean where you can cook—"

"—without building a fucking campfire in the middle of the fucking floor," Riley added.

"That *would* make it a lot nicer," Eddy went on. "Of course, you got your music group there too. I guess that gives you something to *do*."

"That sort of holds things together," Dave admitted.

"Without anything to do," Eddy went on, rolling a screwdriver back and forth across the cab floor with his bare foot, "I guess a commune is just a crash pad. But it could be a nice place. If we could get some lights, even."

"Shit," Riley said. "Then you'd see all them things people are doin' with each other in the dark and there'd go half the fun." At which point he hauled the truck onto the road's shoulder and braked. "Okay, sweetheart, you've had your jollies." Then he looked at Dave and me. "Why don't you guys give a couple of people in the back a chance to breathe for a while, okay?" We'd been driving about two hours. "Time to switch off with some of the others. In fact, I want me some women up here for a while. Three very nice women. Now, go on."

We got down on the road. Gerry, having untied the door, leaned from the van. "What's the matter."

"Just a rest stop," Eddy said.

Dave said: "The driver wants female company."

"Oh, *me!*" Reema said, leaning out beside Gerry.

People came out to stretch. Some of us went off into the bushes to piss.

When I came back, Riley, hanging off the cab's ladder, was saying to Judy, Maxine, Anne, Lady, Reema, and Linda, who clustered below, "Now, you have to choose who's gonna come up here and see the sights with me. Three can sit in the seat. And we can get a fourth in the sleeper if she don't mind peekin' out over my shoulders. But then I ain't so high I'm gonna block the view much."

As I climbed up into the van, I said back over my shoulder: "Your friend Riley's too much."

"He's great," Eddy said, getting his hands in position on the sill. "I love him." He vaulted up behind me.

We sat around the inside, leaning back on the quilting. On the first leg of the trip, some people had tried to play instruments, but the motor was too loud. So when the truck started again, people pretty much just sat. Dominiq came to sit between my legs and lean back on my chest. As things growled and shook around us, she glanced up at me with her round, brown face: "Doesn't it feel like it's going to turn over?"

"No it don't," Gerry said, beside us. "You just ain't ridden in a truck much."

"This is a lot of fun!" Grendahl shouted from across the van. "But does anyone know where we're *going?*"

"It's a monastery," Coca-Cola said. He stood, holding to one of the wall chains and swaying with the van. "I grew up there . . . I lived with the brothers when I was a kid. It's got a waterfall and woods and lots of stuff."

"We're going to a *monastery*?" Dave asked. 'With a *rock group*?"

"It'll be cool," Coca-Cola said. "The brothers won't mind. They like me."

"And your eighteen friends?" Snipper asked.

"It'll be all right," Coca-Cola insisted. "It'll be fine. They're really cool."

16

Riley parked on a small wooded highway.

"Town's right down there," Coca-Cola said when he got out. "We go up this way."

We trooped behind him onto a gravel drive.

Coca-Cola explained that he had to ask permission of the brothers to use the grounds.

We crossed a stone bridge over a fair-sized stream and came out between the high hedges on a couple or three football fields of lawn, patched brown here and there, and with a brazen backing, but looking remarkably good for December.

At the far side was the monastery.

I could see several brothers in brown cassocks, walking across the flags before the main building.

"Come on," Coca-Cola said.

We started walking again.

"Oh, shit! What we must look like to them!" whispered Riley, certainly the most 'normal' looking among us. Still, a couple of times during the ten-minute crossing, the image of cloistered brothers invaded by a gaggle of half-barefoot, half-naked long-hairs got me.

"We have to pray any to use their trees?" Snipper asked.

"Come *on*, now," Eddy said.

Three of the brothers had stopped and were looking.

When we were about twenty feet away, one of the brothers—only a little taller than Riley and not as tall as Snipper—got a funny, surprised expression. He started straight toward us, his hands up. I thought it was some gesture of benediction. But it was just astonishment.

We all stopped walking.

The brother stopped in front of Coca-Cola, reached up, took two handfuls of shaggy blond hair, and exclaimed, "Franklin!" Then he threw back his head, laughing.

It was such a good-humored laugh, we all laughed too. So did the brothers behind him.

"Hello, Brother Francis." Coca-Cola smiled. "I came back to say hello. These are my friends."

"Franklin, what a surprise!" Brother Francis exclaimed. "And all that hair!" Brother Francis, as well as two of the other brothers, was tonsured.

"It's good to see you again," Coca-Cola said. "I came to say hello; and to ask if we could bring our truck around in the back by the waterfall for a while."

"You mean," Brother Francis said, taking Coca-Cola's arm and beginning to walk with him (the rest of us began to walk too), "you wanted to use the grounds, so you thought you'd come by and say hello."

"Hey, Coke!" Riley called from the back of the

group. "He sure as shit got your number!" which left an embarrassed silence.

Brother Francis' laughter, good-humored as before, filled it. "Well, I don't see why not. There are quite a bunch of you, though. . . ."

"We won't make a mess," Coca-Cola said. "We didn't even bring any food. We'll clean up anything we mess up. We have some musicians with us and we're just going to play and listen for a while."

"Musicians? Now, that's nice. You know, there's a dance at the high school this evening, practically across the road from where you'll be. Here . . ." He called to one of the other brothers. "Brother Michael, you remember Franklin, don't you? Or had he left us when you came . . . ?"

And the other brothers fell in beside us as we walked. Two of them were trying not to smile too much.

"Franklin," Brother Francis went on, "what are you doing with yourself now?"

"Not a lot," Coca-Cola said. "I live in a commune now, down in the city."

"A commune?" Brother Francis asked. "Now what, exactly, is that?"

"Well," Coca-Cola said, "it's sort of . . . well, like a monastery. But it's not religious. We live together, share things, take care of one another. We live—well, differently from the people around us."

"I see," Brother Francis said, glancing back. "And all of you live together?"

"No. Some of us live at one commune called the Place. The musicians, though, are from another commune called the Heavenly Breakfast."

"The Heavenly Breakfast," Brother Francis repeated. I couldn't tell from his voice whether he approved or not. We reached the flagstones. "All right. You take your truck and drive around back. And have a good time. Maybe some of us might even come down a little later, and hear some of this music."

"Thanks, Brother Francis!"

The rest of us said thank you too. We walked back across the grass.

A couple of times I glanced at the brothers, who stood together on the patio, watching us.

"Hey." I nudged Lee, who was walking beside me. "Take a look at that."

"Where . . . ?" She glanced around. "Oh—!"

Two (one of whose shaved heads was circled in meager fringe) were miming, with their hands, great hanks of hair while the others swayed with laughter.

17

Riley drove the truck at least half a mile farther, then pulled into a clearing by a stream. (Coca-Cola was up in the cab giving instructions.) Two varnished picnic tables looked as though they'd been set out new that morning.

At various times, in various groups, we followed the stream up a five-tiered falls whose bank rose in rock and scrub perhaps a hundred yards. Once, well into the afternoon, I climbed up by myself, listening to the music of a few people left down by the benches still jamming, stopped, looked across the trees and the far rocks, turned back on the spongy earth, pushed aside branches; and found Lady, alone, sitting on a red, barkless log.

"Hi," I said.

Her fingers, on the close crowns of her knees, meshed awkwardly as dying white spiders. "It's nice here." She moved only her head to look at me.

"Yeah." I nodded.

After a while she asked, "You know how to see twice as far in the forest?"

"How?"

A shaling of winter brown dangled from the branches around us, dotted with tenacious greens.

"Most people . . ." Lady rocked her shoulders, once. "Most city people, when they're in the woods, they just look at the leaves. But look at the spaces *between* the leaves. Pretend they're solids—go on. Look at them as though they were three-dimensional shapes. Stare at them like they were a pile of objects. . . ."

I squinted at the leafy veilings and, while I was trying to do what she said, suddenly had the unnerving experience of seeing the veil clear like a scrim on a theater set, revealing a gully, some boulders, the trunks of other trees, and a slope half-covered with fallen leaves perhaps a hundred feet away.

"Hey . . . !" I laughed a little nervously. "That's really something! It works . . ."

"Now, of course, you'll never be able to see it the other way again," she said. "You'll just get better at this one. Isn't it strange how the things we learn from new experiences change us?" She drew her hands back against the wrinkled cloth at her belly and didn't look at me. "We change—and the whole world changes."

When she didn't say any more, I turned around and climbed down among the trees.

And they were different from when I'd climbed up.

We'd only brought acoustic instruments: two guitars (a small Martin and a large Guild), a banjo—and Lee, her silver flute. With the cases open on the ground, we sat on the tables, tuning.

The way for a group to play a whole afternoon is not to run through the whole repertory at once: all our songs were original and we had a shy double dozen arranged. The way you work it—and if no one tells you, you figure it out after a few times—is for the group to do about three songs. Then someone takes a solo for a half-dozen songs, folk music or popular music that's more familiar. Then the group gets together and does another three. It gives everybody time to relax. The music goes on a lot longer. People feel a lot better about wandering away and wandering back. And the people who want to hear the whole things out (when we got set up, Riley found a tree, sat down with his back against it, hung his arms over his knees, and didn't move for three hours, except to nod at a song he particularly liked) hear more variation.

It's a lot better that way.

The group was coming to the end of Dave's *Rain* when, from behind Riley's juggernaut, inched the headlights, bright bumper, and glistening fender of a late-model Chrysler.

Brother Francis got out and, with his hands in his robe pockets, came over to listen.

When we'd finished (from his tree, Riley nodded), Brother Francis pushed back his brown sleeves and clapped. "Very nice! Very nice!" The others laughed.

"I'd intended," Brother Francis said, "to stay and listen for a while. But I'm afraid I have some work to get back to. You mentioned you didn't have any food with you, so I thought I'd bring by a little something. Will somebody give me a hand?"

"Sure, Father!" Gerry said.

I wondered if that were the way to address a brother.

"It's nothing much," Brother Francis said, preceding Gerry to the car, "but if anyone *is* hungry, it might take the edge off your appetite." Brother Francis opened the back door and Gerry lugged out a green cooler by its aluminum handle.

Eddy wandered up looking curious.

"Lemonade," Brother Francis explained. "And why don't you get those things out," which were three loaves of Italian bread, a net bag of apples, and a wooden box no bigger than a bread loaf, printed with blue and red.

When it was placed on the picnic table, Dave, who had a pocketknife, pried up the top: small tacks gave. Under the wet gauze wrapping, which Reema peeled back, was a translucent yellow cheese.

"Franklin," Brother Francis said, "here, take the trunk keys. There's something in the back of the car for you," and a minute later, the edge wedged against the stomach of his gray sweater, the hole under the collar tugged tightly open by it, Franklin walked stiff-legged to the picnic table, lugging a case of Coca-Cola.

"Hey, hey! That looks great. Brother Francis, I've got a bottle of peach wine here if you'd like some of that . . . ?"

"Well, I . . . no, I think I'll pass it up," Brother Francis said. "But thank you. Really."

The bottles clinked as we pulled them from the case's boarded compartments.

Lee and I took a walk later and she discovered the school where Brother Francis had said the dance would take place. All brick and glass, its cornerstone was dated 1964.

We lounged and explored and drank Cokes and lemonade; and when the sun began to devil the treetops and we'd climbed on the picnic tables for another round of playing, a dozen high-school students, all short-hairs, some in unseasonal Bermuda-length shorts, wandered into the clearing to stand, listening.

Grendahl and Maxine, their arms tucked tight around each other's backs, had wandered back and forth a couple of times. But now, holding the red net bag, a quarter full, Grendahl went over to the school kids. "Any of you want an apple? Come on, take an apple. Go on, if you want. Take some. There's plenty."

Only one of them did, and when he saw his friends didn't, he held his for a whole five minutes before he took a bite.

Between songs, one kid called, "You should come over and play at our dance."

"Naw," another objected. "They wouldn't let 'em in," at which the others laughed. "I mean," he explained, a little flustered, "because they're strangers and they don't have tickets . . ." There was more laughter.

Some of the onlookers drifted away. More drifted over. While I was sitting on the bench, playing, I noticed somebody among them was trying to shush one of the others. Just as I got the feeling there was something going on, there was a loud *clunk*!

Half a dozen of them took off running.

Others fell back.

"What the fuck was that?" Eddy said as Gerry came over.

Snipper, Dave, and Lee stopped playing. I put my guitar in the case at my feet, and stepped over it.

Riley stood up in front of his tree. "Who's messing with the truck, huh?" He came over, slapping dirt from his pants.

I heard one of the town kids whisper, "Come on! Let's go, huh?" Two more started to leave, saw that the others hadn't, and edged back.

On the far side of the truck's cab, high on the door, was a splotch of red. Dribbles ran straight till they hit the aluminum ribbing, built up, then rolled down again to the fender.

The open half-gallon can lay in a puddle on the grass. Red paint had collected around the tire.

"What the *fuck* is *that*?" Eddy said, waving his hands.

The high-school kids stepped back again; some of them were grinning.

"Come on!" Eddy demanded. "What the fuck is *that* supposed to mean?"

Coca-Cola, Joey, Lady, and Little Dave were coming over now. Grendahl and Maxine were behind them.

Riley scratched his neck and looked at the stain, then at the high-school kids.

One of them, with an incredible set of braces, said, "Well . . . since you're hippies, they thought your truck could use a little color." Some of the others laughed again. "They just figured to help you paint it."

Riley kept looking back and forth between the truck and the kids. For a moment I thought perhaps he was waiting for something from us to define the appropriate reaction from his newly adopted life-style.

"That was pretty nice of you guys," Dave, who was about the biggest person there, said. "Now you've had your fun, why don't you just fuck off, huh?"

"We didn't throw it," one of them said. He smiled. Another one said, "Ain't you gonna play no more?"

Dave just shook his head and walked away. The rest of us followed. Riley, the last, glanced a few more times, then came on.

"We got some turp back at the Breakfast," Dave said, putting his hand on the little truck driver's shoulder. "We can wipe it down now and clean it good when we get back to the city."

"A little paint ain't gonna hurt the way she runs." Riley shrugged his shoulders under Dave's hand and glanced back again.

A kid with an apple core in one hand was leading the others from the clearing. He saw us look, tossed the core away into the trees—I saw where it landed—and they filed out.

"I might," Riley said, and laughed, "just leave it. You know, the first battle scar?"

But that was the end of the Breakfast music for the evening. There was talk of leaving right away, but half of the people were up at the top of the waterfall. And before they came back, others had wandered off. So we hung around another hour and a half till it began to get dark.

Grendahl and Maxine were sitting at one of the benches, their arms around each other, occasionally talking, occasionally kissing.

Eddy was leaning against the tree. Riley walked over, slipped under Eddy's arm and put his head on Eddy's pockmarked chest. "Hey, sweetheart," Riley said, looking up. "Don't be so glum; gimme a kiss." Eddy dropped his face on Riley's upturned one; Riley's arms came up around Eddy's neck. After a while they walked away together.

"Hey." Lee came up behind me. "I want to show you something."

I followed her back into the woods, where I climbed behind her to the second tier of the falls, so close to the water, the spray wet our shoulders. Climbing, she jerked her flute awkwardly beside her till, suddenly, from the top of the silver wand, gold spilled down it, snagging keys.

I looked behind me.

The sun, up here, was still up, in salmon, its height again from the horizon.

"Now, listen," Lee said, backing under a branch that brushed spotted leaves over her hair. She blew a clutch of notes, faltered.

A sharp echo tumbled them back at us a whole second and a half after the flute left her lips.

"Wait a minute," she said. "Let me see if I can get this right. I made it work before . . ." She raised her chin and her flute.

A leaf staggered on her hair.

"What . . . ?" I began.

"I wrote a round," she explained. "It's only a three-note delay. But I have to get the time perfect." She pulled in her chin, rolled the mouth plate on her lower lip.

The notes shot across the water's hiss. When they returned, a second and a half later, she'd move a third away.

Lee, and her echo, played.

She continued through the six-measure melody and at the end modulated to a key a diminished fourth higher; her echo, in perfect consonance, followed.

"God*damn.* . . !" I said.

She kept playing.

Snipper was coming down the rocks. As he neared, he frowned at us, realized what he was hearing—a couple others were behind him—and stopped, with an expression much odder than any frown I'd ever seen.

Dave, Grendahl, Maxine, and Gerry were climbing up.

Lee had one sneaker on a log, tapping time.

Gerry, after looking around—you could tell he was trying to see the other player—suddenly realized what she was doing, ran his hand through his stubby little braids, and said, "Wow! Oh, wow! Wow!" Then he tried to bop to the music and snap his fingers. It wasn't really finger-popping music. But he kept on till Riley, behind him, said:

"Nigger, will you shut up!"

So he did. It almost blew Lee's cool anyway. But she finished, having worked twice through all three possible keys. She took the flute away from her mouth and looked astoundingly happy.

Three terminal notes returned.

"Jesus," Snipper said. "*What* was that? I mean, what *was* that?"

"What do you call it?" Grendahl asked.

"I don't know," Lee said. "What's the name of this place, anyway?"

Coca-Cola was sitting on the end of the log where Lee had been tapping her foot. "St. Amory Falls." He slid his bare feet through loud leaves.

"I could call it that," Lee said.

From under Grendahl's arm, Maxine, putting her glasses back on, said, "Sounds to me more like St. Amory Rises."

Among the laughs, Lee's was a veritable cackle.

(Which is how *St. Amory Rises* got named.)

"You know," Maxine said, "Lady's lying down in the back of the van."

"She all right?" Gerry asked.

"Just tired. But it's going to be dark in a little while. Perhaps we should think about starting back?" And since that was the twelfth time someone had said that in the last hour and a half, with the sun, we went down.

While Riley started the truck, we were still lashing back the door inside the van so it would stay open. Then we sat along the padded wall opposite while branches caught, and snapped, and slapped the jamb, and hinges tore at leaves.

Black trees pulled ragged across blue.

There were a few moments of light through glass walls and over brick, silhouetting a dozen-odd youngsters (in overcoats now, for December had suddenly reasserted itself) milling before the high school. Over their rackety PA, the Beatles sang: "You say, 'Goodbye,' and I say, 'Hello . . . ! Hello! Hello!' I don't know why . . ."

Cushioned on the diesel's thunderous hum, we rumbled back to the city.

18

Janice bore Tap (she named him after her grand-
father, Tappen) when she was seventeen, in South
Dakota. By way of San Francisco, Mexico City, Winni-
peg, and Coconut Grove, she had made her way, with
her son, to New York, where she first met Billy, who
had the biggest feet of anyone I'd ever seen—five-foot-
six, he'd worn holes in the sides and toes of size-
thirteen-and-a-half U.S. Keds in three weeks—very
green eyes, and a gentle but persuasive way about
dealing dope. A little over a year later, Janice bore
Caleb, who, when I met him, age three, had Billy's
eyes; and was on his way to filling Billy's shoes. Ac-
cording to Little Dave, whose friends they were, Billy
had spent the last thirteen months somewhere else
while Janice collected welfare on Ninth Street. He'd
come back two months ago. Janice had then been six
months pregnant.

They came around often, at first visiting Little
Dave, then just visiting in general, quiet usually, smiling mostly, one under the arm of the other. Reema
took to going over to use Janice's sewing machine.
And finally Billy went in with (Big) Dave and Grendahl on one of their more-complicated grass deals. So
they were pretty much part of the family.

One morning while they were eating with us, Joey
asked, doffing his bottle, "You want a boy or a girl?"

"Doesn't matter, long as it's healthy," Billy said

from the arm of the easy chair. "And doesn't cry much."

"Caleb didn't cry much," Janice said, sitting forward on the easy-chair cushion, her plate far out on her knees. "Neither did Tap."

"You have some pretty kids," Joey said.

Little Dave, at the stove, was spooning down seconds from last night's beef stew to Tap, who held his plate at about his nose.

Billy grinned, leaned forward, put one hand over Janice's belly, and with the other took Joey's wine. "This one's going to be just as pretty as the others, too." He downed a swig, frowned without really stopping his grin, and handed the bottle back.

"It's probably going to have brown eyes," Janice said. "I'm pretty sure his dad had brown eyes—I thought it might have been Little Dave's. Anyway"—and she started to push Billy's hand away—"whoever it is, his old man's Puerto Rican"—but changed her mind and held it by the thumb.

"We're going to have three pretty kids," Billy said. "One with blue eyes, one with green eyes, and one with brown eyes. I think that's nice."

Tap took his plate to the middle of the floor, bent over and put it in front of Caleb, who sat cross-legged on the linoleum. "You can have some of this too," Tap said.

Caleb, both fists joined beneath his chin, looked for a while. Then he picked out a chunk of meat with one hand, tasted it carefully, then, with the other hand, picked out a second chunk, and, just as carefully, tasted that.

Janice watched them, sliding her arms across the back of Billy's hand.

Two weeks later, Billy was busted.

The next morning at six-forty-seven, pushing things to the verge of soap opera, Janice went into labor and was ambulanced to Bellevue.

That afternoon, Reema stopped by Janice and Billy's apartment on Ninth to collect some things to take up to the hospital. She found the door broken in, the place looted. While she was standing in the middle of the vandalized living room, the landlord came in and began to yell at her—something about the police having broken into the apartment that morning looking for drugs; they had found nothing, apparently, but had left the place wide open. Looters had done the rest. The landlord went on to shout at Reema that he was going to padlock the door, that he wanted the goddamn hippies out, newborn baby or no—moving things into first-class melodrama, a fact each new batch at the Breakfast who heard the tale commented on.

It was three days after Christmas.

"I think I wanted to kill him," Reema said, pacing the kitchen. When she'd come in, she'd been crying. "I really did. All he cares about is avoiding any fucking problems for him!"

The bust, at least, turned out to be a false alarm.

Billy was released after five days because he'd been mistaken for someone else, or because there was no evidence, or because somebody had lost what evidence there was. No one quite got it straight.

At any rate, Janice, Tap, Caleb, Billy, and four-day-old daughter all came to stay at the Heavenly Breakfast on Thursday morning, December 28th, 1967.

"I named her after Billy," Janice said, leaning away from the blanket bundle to open the toaster. "I thought that would be nice."

Bent over a cup of coffee, Billy turned from the stove, the steaming rim invisible inside his fingers. "I think that's going to be confusing." He sipped.

"We'll call her Willy, then," Janice said. "I just like you so much, I wanted two of you around."

"Can't knock that, I guess." Billy grinned through the steam. "Come on," he said to Tap, who was swinging on his free hand and standing on Billy's bare feet, "don't make me spill this, now."

"You like Janice's new baby?" Tap asked.

Billy gave a considered nod. "I think it's pretty good, as babies go. What about you?"

Tap considered too, while Janice hefted the small dark head against her shoulder. Finally he nodded.

"Come on, Tap," Janice said. "Here's some toast. Go get the peanut butter."

Little Dave was sitting on the easy chair and Caleb was sitting on Little Dave's knee, plucking at the nylon guitar strings while Little Dave fingered the chords. Every time Caleb got three notes together, he'd laugh loudly, and all of us would look over and smile.

I was astonished how much I enjoyed this month Janice and family were there.

When I've lived *seul*, *à deux*, or even *à trois*, the prospect of parents visiting with their kids was never my favorite. Baby-proofing an apartment—making sure all small movable objects are over five feet off the ground—is a drag. But at the Breakfast, there were enough people to keep an eye on the kids with no sweat. Also, they were happy, bright, creative children and they added their own thing to the commune.

After the first rehearsal, Tap informed us he had given up all plans to be a fireman and had decided instead to be a pop-music star. After the second, Tap, Caleb, and Willy seemed quite capable of ignoring all noise entirely.

Snipper decided he was going to help Tap learn to read, and discovered that Caleb practically knew how already. So one of the little rooms, for a couple of hours every day, became a classroom.

We put a mattress in the little room for Tap and Caleb, who, if anything, were delighted to have so many adults around to pay attention to them. And I remember Janice laughing one afternoon when she,

63

Billy, Reema, and caligrapher Bob had come back
from a display of Oriental graphics at the Metropoli-
tan Museum, saying, "I never knew having kids could
be this much fun. I don't even see them half the day!"

Other than Electric Baby's stay, this was the only
time there were children living at the Heavenly
Breakfast. Janice and Billy were with us just over a
month. No one had thought of the place particularly
in terms of children, but we all, I think, began to see
the possibility for child-rearing.

19

The commune we were closest to, of course, was Summer, in New Jersey. There was Chip, who had the
same name I did, wore an earring through his left ear-
lobe like I did, but had bright red hair. (Mine is
black.) There was Candy and her dog, Candy's Dog;
and Jonah, who made clothes; and Joan, who made
pots; and Big Bobby, who'd inherited the run-down
New Jersey farmhouse from an uncle and had left off
studying architecture to fix it up; and the thin twins,
Lenn and Saxon. I was always delighted when either
or both of their microbuses—the one with the psychedelic paint job was called Pumpkin, and the other,
still its original factory blue, was Fred—pulled up
across from the firehouse by our stoop. And if practically anyone else in the Breakfast were writing this and
talking about our encounters with other communal
groups, Summer would be the one they would talk
about most.

I never got there.

Almost anytime when you hadn't seen Snipper or Anne or Little Dave for a day or two, it was because they'd braved the January chills and hitched down to Summer. Dozens of times large groups, ferried by Fred or Pumpkin, went back and forth. We had standing invitations with each other. Still, somehow I was never up to hitching in the cold, or around when a ride left.

But there was one other commune beside the Place, though, the Breakfast met.

I never even learned their name, if they had a name.

I first became aware of them through an account of Phyllis'. She was one of Little Dave's girlfriends and had stayed over a few times.

". . . living across the hall from me, like a biker gang or something!" She sat at the red-checked table, drinking tea. "Only they didn't have any bikes—except maybe one of them, I think. They terrorized the whole apartment house. Christ, they drove *me* out. Really, they're the reason I moved. And *I* got along pretty well with them! You know, I came home one evening from work and they'd broken into my apartment and taken practically everything! It was funny, really. I had no idea *they'd* done it, and I went running across the hall to knock on their door and see if they'd heard anybody breaking in. I walked into their place—which you'd have to see to believe—and there was my clock-radio, right on the windowsill in front of the gate. And on the other side of the room was my television! I began to march around their apartment looking: they had my *hair* dryer in the back room!"

"What did you *do*?" Reema asked.

"I made them carry it all back. I told them, 'Come on. This is ridiculous.' And I made them take everything back into my apartment. Including the hair dryer. And two chairs they'd walked off with. And some tools."

"Did you ask them why they'd broken in?"

"I didn't want to *know*!" Phyllis said. "They had this big red swastika painted on the door. I mean, I'm not religious or anything, but I was born Jewish. It was a little unnerving to come out of my apartment to *that* every morning on my way to work. And I'm sure at least *one* of them is Jewish too."

"Maybe," Little Dave said, pouring some tea for himself and coming to the table, "they think that makes the swastika all right."

"It just makes it sicker," Phyllis said, "if you ask me. And the noise that would come out of that place! Yelling and music and shrieking and I don't know what all. Why the police weren't up there three times a week, *I'll* never know."

"At least they gave your stuff back."

"Oh, like I said, in our own peculiar way we got along very well. For a while. You know: smile and nod in the halls, 'Hello, how are you, what's happening, that's nice.' And they'd go hulking on up the steps; boots, chains, half the time no shirts; perfectly filthy, most of them—also, most of them are rather little too—and that would be all you'd see of them. They had one or *two* big ones. . . ."

"If they broke into your apartment, why did they give your stuff back?"

"I think," Phyllis said, looking at the dark leaves in her teacup, "it's because they aren't very bright. One of them installed the new lock on my door to replace the one they'd broken."

"Did they pay for it?"

"No, dear. *I* paid for it. I didn't want to push my luck. But one of them did install it. Then I heard some stories about some kid they killed. Or at least some people *said* they'd killed him. Up at Galahad's." The original Diggers commune was going then and still getting a lot of publicity. "They just walked in and beat some kid within an inch of his life. With chains. I know he went into the hospital. And somebody said he died. Anyway, that's when I decided to move. I mean, they were shooting guns through the goddamn walls. Really. A gun went off in their place and the bullet went right through the floor into the apartment below. Nobody was hurt. But somebody could have been. Then Gladys told me about an apartment in her building—a nice, safe, locked building on Twelfth. I moved that week and figured I was lucky."

"Did they help you move too?" Little Dave asked.

"I started getting my stuff out at four o'clock in the morning precisely so they shouldn't know I was leaving till I was long gone." Phyllis looked over at the teapot still on the stove, contemplating another cup. "A lot of good *that* did me! I mean, they're in and out at all hours anyway. I kept running into them on the stairs."

20

In the Tompkins Square library one morning, I came across an article in a psychology journal that puzzled me; I brought my puzzlement back to the Breakfast.

When we had finished rehearsal that afternoon, I went in the back, where Janice was getting ready to nurse Willy. "Janice," I asked, "I read this article that was talking about how kids, for the first couple of months, get all upset and start crying and everything, every time Mom starts to ball—even if the kid is sleeping in another room on the other side of the house."

"It's true," Janice said. "Even if you don't make a sound, too. It's enough to make you believe in telepathy."

"Then what's with Willy here?" I asked. "You guys go at it enough, but once Willy falls out, I don't hear a peep all night."

Janice laughed. "Oh, Billy figured out what to do about that back when we first had Caleb." She unbuttoned the shoulder of the paisley nursing blouse Reema had made for her. "If you put them in bed *with* the two of you, so they have something warm to curl up against, I guess it's like bouncing them in a baby carriage or something. They sleep right through." She adjusted her nipple with a finger on either side. "There's another thing about having them in bed, it turns your old man on something terrible. Really. If I want to ball, Billy can be sound asleep, and all I have to do is push Willy up against him, and—" She snapped her fingers. "Like that! It's certainly a lot better than you being horny and having the kid shrieking. I learned that one back with Tap's old man. Just thank God for rubber pants."

"Oh," I said, scratching my head. "The article didn't have a solution."

"They ought to," Janice said. "I'm sure it would save a lot of people a lot of problems."

Janice and Billy finally took an apartment two houses down the block. It hadn't bothered the children, but I think a three-hour rock rehearsal every day would have to get to just about anybody else. Once they moved, they were still in and out a lot. Sometimes they left the kids with us for baby-sitting. I think all of us at the Breakfast felt like adopted uncles and aunts, or perhaps some closer relation that hasn't been given a name yet.

21

So many incidents: so many people.

Once they were fixed by the ordering of real time.

Now, cut loose in memory with only notebook references for data—those, for the most part, undated or scarce of detail—they come together in a new mosaic.

Judy had her sixteenth birthday during one of the weeks she stayed at the Breakfast. The girl shot amazing amounts of speed—I doubt I ever saw her when she wasn't whacked. Still, she was pretty in a pink-plump sort of way, and almost phlegmatic in her personality—which is so unusual in a speed freak I have a note to myself to suggest to her that she see a doctor to find out if her phenomenal intake over a year and a half did not have some physiological basis.

I made that suggestion several times.

I don't know if she ever took it.

Every few weeks she returned to her home in Queens for a couple of days. When she came back to the Lower East Side, she brought horrifying tales of her homelife, vicious with howling, hair-pulling fights with her mother; at home her mother called the police on her regularly. "Most of the time, now, they won't come. She never wants them for anything—she tells them to put me in jail because I've just come back from running away. The awful thing is, in some weird way she probably loves me. Sometimes, when she's calm, she says she likes me to come see her. That's the only reason I go. Then she starts hitting me.

If it's just for the exercise, I wish she'd lift weights."
Judy was exorbitantly intelligent. "I want to get as
high as possible and stay that way as long as possible.
I want to have as little to do as I can with what's
real," she would say with all seeming innocence, leaning on the doorjamb of the small room where Little
Dave perched on his stool inside, the signal light of
his soldering gun pink on his chin, nose, the ceiling of
his eye sockets; he was overhauling Big Dave's
secondhand amp, purchased from someone staying at
Third and Second Avenue with the Dead.

"Oh, come on," Snipper would say to her. "Sure, it's
nice, but . . ." And the argument would begin.

She waited for it and came back at it with a cyni-
cism that would have been scarey had she not presented her defense with the charm Shaw loaned to
Barbara, to Cleopatra—peppered with quotes from
Kierkegaard, whom she was reading busily and pas-
sionately that month. She was one of the terrible children who never makes a grammatical mistake.

We laughed a good deal about it; we argued a good
deal—till Little Dave told us to shut up and go to the
other side of the kitchen.

Judy conceded points to us, as good debaters will;
the evidence, to her, was overwhelmingly on her side,
if only by its profusion. Eventually, still laughing, we
began to see it as tragic, if only by its coercive order.

22

Phil Blumberg was a clerk in the East Side Book Store. Crossing St. Mark's Place, I would usually stop in to break away from the cold. Over the cash register, Phil and I had had a couple of conversations. He discovered first that he was selling some books I had once written, then that I lived in a commune.

"So do I," he exclaimed, with delight. "It's called January House—up near Columbia University . . . ?" He wore glasses and had a beach ball of curly auburn hair. "I've only been there for three months, but the commune itself has been going for years. It started as a group who were interested in Buddhist studies back in the fifties—it had some connection with International House. But now they've gotten out of all that. And they just go along. Say, why don't you come up and visit us? You'd probably find it interesting. We could give you dinner."

I'd been telling him a little about the Heavenly Breakfast, and I somehow just assumed his 'you' was plural. "We'd really like that," I said. "Just tell us when you want us to come."

"Well . . ." Phil smiled. "Why don't you just bring *a* friend. I don't know if we could handle a whole invasion."

"Oh," I said. "Well, sure. What would be a good day?"

"Maybe tomorrow . . . no, that's when Dan is cooking. I cook on Thursdays, but that's no great

shakes. It always comes out spaghetti no matter what
I start out to make."

"I don't mind spaghetti," I offered.

"Make it Saturday," Phil said, leaning his elbows on
the pile of invoices stacked on the counter. "Yeah,
that'll be best."

"Okay," I said.

"At six-thirty."

"Saturday," I repeated. "At six-thirty. With a friend."

Back at the Breakfast, I asked Lee, "You want to go
to dinner Saturday at six-thirty?"

She turned down the tap, looked at me a little
strangely, and swirled the washcloth in the water by
her hip. "Sure," she said after a moment, "why not?"
and began to soap under her arm.

23

The three-story house was sandwiched between aging
walk-up apartments. Inside the vestibule were the
twin doors of a two-family house. There was a bell on
each, but only one number on the outside door.

I looked at Lee, shrugged, and rang the bell on the
left.

Somebody came running up behind the door on the
right. His shadow swung over the curtain behind the
glass; the door opened and Phil said, "Hi! You made
it!" and backed against the hall wall so we could enter. "Just go on down—there! That's my room," he said
as we were about to walk past.

Phil pushed open the door and we went in.

On both sides of the fireplace were bookshelves. Beside the daybed, with its purple corduroy spread, was a hi-fi. I saw the speakers on opposite sides of the room. "I lucked out getting this room," Phil said. "It's chilly when it gets really cold. But other than that, I think it's the nicest room on this floor. A couple of other people here would have liked to get it, but . . ." He shrugged, smiling. On the wall were posters of the Cream and Moby Grape—not commercial ones manufactured for the poster shops, but ones that had been in display cases outside concert halls. "This is really a very interesting place. We have quite an interesting group here. You'll probably meet some of them as the evening goes on." He'd been sitting on the bed; but now he bounced up. "Would you like the tour?"

Just as Lee said, "Sure—" a tall guy, in a marine shirt open over a sunken chest, a beer bottle in one hand, very blue eyes, and skin the color of regular coffee when they're short on milk, leaned into the room: "Hi, Phil. How's it going?"

"Hey, Sam," Phil said. "This is Chip. And his girl-friend . . . ?"

"Lee," Lee introduced herself when it got her turn to shake hands.

"Say," Sam said, "maybe after dinner we could come in and listen to your record player? You know, I don't have one, and a couple of friends of mine called up and said they had some records they wanted me to hear."

"Sure," Phil said.

"I'll bring over some beer. By the way, would someone like a swig of this?"

"I would," Lee said.

"It beats peach wine," I told him, and took a swallow.

"Thanks," Phil said. "But I'm really not into alcohol. Just pot. Not that I have anything *against* alcohol. I'm just not into it."

73

When Sam offered us seconds, I think Lee and I both decided we liked him. At the door, he bobbed his bottle, and left.

"He's a really good guy," Phil said. "But he's going through a really funny period. He was separated from his wife a couple of years ago and he's trying to get custody of his two children. He says she's crazy. She probably is; but he's a little crazy too, sometimes. Come on, I'll show you the place."

The halls, in the light of the naked bulb hanging near the bathroom door, were a pale green just distinguishable from gray.

"I gotta take a piss," I said, and went in the bathroom. Lee closed the door behind me; I'd forgotten. I stepped over a yellow plastic cat box that held about half of a ten-pound bag of kitty litter. My boots ground on the spillage.

On the bathtub bottom were those rubber flowerforms they put down to keep you from slipping. On the back of the toilet were bottles—of turquoise shampoo; one of gold bath oil; another of pink salts. The toilet paper, tied to the wall with a string, was the crinkly kind. I could tell without feeling it.

I pissed, flushed, and trod back to the door over kitty litter.

"Clarice has cats," Phil explained when I came out. "That's Clarice's room." Thumbtacked to the closed door was a picture of a mandala from a magazine about *Life* size. "Sam's in there."

From another door, open, came guitar music. As we passed, a woman smiled out and swung it shut.

"That's Sybil's room; hers and her husband's—well, he's not really her husband, but he might as well be. They're teachers in the Craft Center." We moved on. "And there's a television room in the back, right around here . . ." The hall bent, then opened into a room with a sofa, some wall shelves (I saw two of my books among the paperbacks; I liked that), a coffee table, and a TV. "Nobody really uses it much, though. Sam's got a TV in his room, but no hi-fi. You want to go and see upstairs?"

"Sure," I said.

"We have to go out of the house and through the other entrance," Phil explained. "There's no stairway inside between the floors."

We followed him back past the closed doors. We went out the front one into the cold vestibule—the sky had been dark blue before; now it was black—and after Phil unlocked the door beside it into a narrow, green-gray stairwell. We followed Phil up while he jangled his keys against his leg.

As we reached the head of the stairs, a rotund bald man with a beard, in mattress-ticking overalls, came into the hall.

"Hi, Lief," Phil said. "This is Chip, and . . . ?"

"Lee," Lee said.

"Lee," said Phil.

"Hello," Lief said and shook our hands. "You're Phil's dinner guests? How come everyone invites guests on the nights I'm cooking, but nobody invites anybody on the nights that, say, Dan or . . . Clarice cooks?"

Phil laughed. "Because you cook better than Dan. Or Clarice."

"The only reason," said Lief, "they don't cook well is that they don't like to cook in the first place. It's very simple." His voice was sepulchral, a little arrogant; but the laugh that followed it was friendly enough. "Well, let me get back to my hot stove and do some more slaving." He marched up the hall.

"That's Lief's room." Phil pointed to the door that Lief had closed after him when he'd entered the hall. "He's a painter. He's been here longer than anybody else. Almost ten years. There're a couple of people who've been here two or three. But seven or eight months seems to be the average."

"Transients are all downstairs," Lee suggested, "and permanent residents up here?"

"It sort of works out that way, I guess," Phil said. "Wait . . . no. Dan's room is up here. And he's just been here six weeks. Of course, he's been a friend of Lief's for . . . well, an awfully long time. But we all vote on the new people who come in. And, back just after I got here, we voted somebody out. Lief says that's the first time it's every happened since the place started. He was sort of upset about having to do it. But the guy was just crazy."

"Why'd you want him out?" Lee asked.

"Well"—Phil laughed—"for one thing, he tried to make everybody in the commune. I don't mean just the girls. The guys too."

"What's wrong with that?" I asked.

"Hell," Phil said. "That wasn't the main reason, I guess. I mean, Lief is gay . . . *I'm* gay. Nobody was *shocked* or anything. Everybody around here is pretty cool." He shook his head a little. "He just went about it in the wrong tone of voice. You know what I mean?"

Lee nodded.

"It's like he thought living in a commune should be all free love, free dope . . . It's just not what people were interested in here. You know?" Phil put his hands in his pockets. "Too bad, he was sort of cute. And interesting—in his way." We walked with Phil up the hall. "I only really saw him a couple of times. When I got here, the situation was pretty sticky. Sometimes, I think they took me in just to get somebody who would put in another vote against him. Some of the people who're gone now thought that he should stay, no matter how unpleasant he was. But Lief, who really pretty much runs things, figured he just wouldn't work out. He was probably right."

"Say," I said, as we entered a dining room mostly

filled with a large table, "how do you work things here like rent?"

"Well," Phil explained, "there're six people downstairs and four people upstairs, and the rent on the whole house is two hundred a month. We each pay twenty-five a month for rent, which you have to admit is pretty fine for New York." He pulled out a chair. There were already napkins laid around the table. "Have a seat. . . . Then we throw in another six dollars a week for food. That's dinner, and dry cereal, fruit and stuff for breakfast."

"That does sound like a pretty good deal," Lee said, sitting in the chair at the head of the table.

I put my hands in my pockets and leaned my butt on the sideboard.

"I've never heard of a better one," Phil said. "How much does each person pay at your place?"

"Well . . ." I began.

Just then a girl in black jeans and a very red sweater came through the room, patted Phil's shoulder (he grinned up and patted her hand back) and went into the kitchen: "Lief, do you want a hand?"

"Yes. But it will not get you out of your turn washing dishes."

"*I* wash dishes tonight," Phil called in to the kitchen.

"I know," Lief called back. "But Beverly dries."

"Jesus!" Beverly said. "I'm just trying to be friendly!"

"There, there," Lief said. "I didn't mean anything. Why don't you take the salad in?"

Beverly came back in with a great wooden bowl, which must have held two gallons of pale- and deep-green lettuce, up against her bright sweater (Beverly herself was very black) and set it on the table.

I was listening to Lief clink pots, and looking at the children's crayon drawings tacked to the walls, and trying to decide whether to divide seventy-five dollars

77

a month by ten, twelve, or fifteen. But Phil seemed to have forgotten his question.

Lief, a towel in one hand and a pot top in the other, stepped into the kitchen doorway. "It's six-thirty. Why don't you go call people for dinner?"

Which Phil went off to do.

"You look uncomfortable," Lee said.

"Me?"

"Mmmm." Lee nodded.

But people were coming up the stairs, coming in, pulling out their chairs, laughing with one another, taking their seats. I had Sam on one side and Phil on the other. Lee sat across from me.

Lief carried in a smoking casserole, its handles on each side bunched in toweling.

When Sybil cut the toasted crumb topping with the large spoon that had a white ceramic handle painted with blue flowers, so much steam came out she jumped back.

Everyone laughed.

Pasta and onions and eggplant and chicken and shrimp: "It's fantastic," everybody said.

"It really is," Beverly agreed. But she was picking out the shrimp with her fork and nudging them to the back of her plate.

"By the way," Phil said loudly as someone handed me the salad, "these are my guests this evening, Chip and . . . ?"

"Lee," Sam said from my other side.

Everybody said hello and told us their names in a ring, and we laughed about not being able to remember them; only, I did. Then the conversation went back to Dan's job, to Sam's inability to find one, and the varied cross-converse of people who know each other well.

I ate pretty quietly.

So did Lee.

Dan, perhaps twenty-five and the one short-haired

man at the table (discounting Lief, who was just bald), said to Lee:

"Phil tells us you live in a commune too?"

"That's right." Lee took another forkful of salad.

"I like these one-big-happy-family arrangements," Dan said, addressing the last of that to me. "Don't you find it gives you so much more of a sense of community? Of course I've just been here a few weeks. And I've never done anything like this before. But it's been great so far. It really has. It's just great for someone like me."

I smiled and nodded and did feel uncomfortable.

"I think," Lief said from the foot of the table, "the commune is much the best replacement for the family. I'm glad to hear that so many others are springing up. I haven't had a chance to visit too many, but from what I hear, though, some of them could stand a little more organization. They're always breaking up so quickly. And of course that's what critics of our kind of life-style are so fast to jump on. But I feel something like a shining example. January House has been here ten years now."

Sam said, with a smile that was pretty much for himself, "I don't know if the commune is a replacement for the family; but it's a nice way to live. The family, the commune, each has its own thing." I recalled what Phil had said about the situation with Sam's kids.

"I don't see why communes couldn't replace the nuclear family," Lief insisted, in the tone of someone who'd said precisely this to this group many times. "I'd certainly like to see it. Communes can be made very stable with a little planning. Well, there . . ." Lief looked at me. "What do you think? Do you think communes should replace the ordinary family life-style?"

"Maybe," I said. "But . . ." and couldn't figure out how to articulate what I wanted to say.

Lief laughed and crumpled his napkin on the black-and-white bib of his overalls. "You see? You see, it never fails. But," he said, "why are you young ones all so conservative? You'll come down and live in a place like this for a year or so. But you're just playing. You're not *really* willing to give up the security of the isolated nuclear family. You always go back to it. . . . I just hope something rubs off while you're here and you can take it with you. Oh, now, here! Don't look so glum. I'm just going on! Really!" and Lief laughed again.

The conversation went on to Clarice's cats, to Sam's inadequate dish-drying, to Sybil's gig folk-singing in a coffeehouse-restaurant near Columbia.

After cut-up fruit and sour cream, and a while standing around the kitchen trying to help Phil wash ("We'll dry . . . ?"

("No," Beverly said. "It really *is* my turn. And if you guys do it, Lief'll just get upset. Sharing the work evenly is one of the big things around here."), we went downstairs, out one door, into the other, and back to Phil's room.

I sat on the bed.

Phil sat in the big chair.

Lee squatted in front of the bookshelf beside the fireplace.

I looked at the wrinkle Phil's pants leg made across his knee, at a dust boll by the rug, at the cracks in the enamel on the thumbtack head on the lower-left-hand corner of the Cream poster.

"Well," Phil said, "how do you like our setup?"

Lee had found a book, and sat cross-legged on the floor now, reading. Her sneaker had folded the rug.

"It's a pretty nice bunch of people," I said.

"I'm really happy I found this place. It's good to live in a place where the people care about each other."

I nodded. "It's a little formal, though."

Phil frowned, considering. "Well, I guess when people live this close, they have certain experiences in common; they know certain things about each other; and we tend to talk about them. . . ."

I frowned back; then I realized he was referring to how little, other than Lief's joking speech, anyone had talked to us at dinner.

"I understand that," I said. It hadn't bothered me, really. "I just mean there's a sort of college-fraternity-house quality about this place here that's—"

"Oh, now, *wait* a minute!" Phil uncrossed his legs and leaned forward. "Look, I *lived* in a college fraternity house, and it isn't like this at all!" He was smiling, but it was a puzzled smile.

Lee glanced up from her book a moment, then turned the page.

I couldn't think of anything else to do, so I laughed. "It's a very nice place," I said. "But it's very different from our . . . commune."

I wanted to describe the Breakfast. But though I'd mentioned aspects of it to people, this was the first time I'd felt compelled to organize my description. I had no idea where to start, nor where to go once started.

"This is supposed to be one of the best," Phil was saying, clearly concurring with whoever had made the assessment.

I was still wondering how to begin saying what I wanted to say when the door swung open, and Sam, a quart beer bottle in each hand, leaned into the room. "Hi!" he said. "My friends got here. We thought we'd come in and listen to some records . . . ?" He waited to see if Phil's invitation was still good. Out in the hall someone was laughing very loudly and stepping around a lot.

"Sure," Phil said.

Sam came in.

The guy behind, who was very thin and had scapula-length brown hair, carried a chair.

The guy behind him, with longer hair and three more bottles of beer, was still laughing.

Sam clinked his bottles down by the bed—"I'll get the records!"—and ducked out again.

The other two stood in the middle of the floor.

"Put those down there," Phil said, pointing somewhere vaguely. "Have a seat. My name's Phil."

"I'm Frank," the one with the bottles said. "That's Jim."

Jim put down his chair, sat in it, and smiled.

Frank hefted his armful of bottles. "Sam thought we could come in here, maybe, and listen to a little music? Maybe trade a little juice for a little smoke, too?"

Phil stood up and went to his desk. "I'll sit out on the beer. But you're welcome to some smoke."

Frank hooted appreciatively and swayed.

I got up, took two of the bottles from him (he was pretty drunk already, I realized) and put them down near the others by the bed.

"That's Chip," Phil said, taking papers and a baggie full of grass from the drawer.

"Lee," Lee said, looking up from her book again, before Phil had a chance to register having forgotten her name again.

"How you doing?" Frank said, extending his hand, palm up.

I was supposed to slap it.

So I did. "Fine, thanks."

Sam came back in. "Here we go. Jimmy and Frank brought these over. I haven't heard them yet. But they look like a gas." With his free hand he took the plastic top off the turntable.

"You know how to work that," Phil said, carrying joint junk back to his chair.

"Sure."

A guitar soared out with the harsh sound that the

media, only a few months ago, had labeled acid rock.

"Isn't that amazing?" Frank demanded. "Just amazing? Jimmy, you ever heard this one before?"

"Yeah," Jimmy said from his chair. "It's great."

Sam sat on the bed, reached down, opened a beer bottle, and passed it to me.

Frank stepped back a little, and Jim slid his chair forward about a foot, which formed us all, including Lee, who was still reading, into a circle; everyone's head, though, was at a different level.

"You gotta listen to this," Frank repeated. "This is really unbelievable. You know, I first heard these guys play out in . . ." And when it became clear Frank wasn't going to give anyone a chance to listen, because he wanted to tell the story of his last six months' adventures (Lee looked at the record player a couple of times, then back to her book), Sam broke in to explain: "Frank's a poet. A pretty good one, too. But he's had a little too much, maybe." He smiled apologetically. "Phil showed me some of your books; we have 'em in the back. Maybe if you read some of his stuff—" Sam nodded toward the unsteady Frank, who was still talking—"he wouldn't seem so strange."

"Frank isn't strange." I grinned. "Just enthusiastic." The music shrieked and rumbled.

"Yeah," Sam said. "I guess that's what it is."

Phil finished rolling a third joint (two others lay on the easy-chair arm), ran it in and out of his mouth, lit it, took a toke and, lips tight and eyes wide, leaned over to hand it to Lee.

"Hey!" Sam said, breaking in on Frank's monologue. "Hey! Chip's a writer. He lives in a commune too, down in the East Village."

"Yeah?" Frank asked, swinging around, then swung back to Phil. "Say, you ever see the guy you used to have staying here? The one you all ganged up on and kicked out? A pretty strange cat! I ran into him about a week ago downtown. Had a pretty nice time together, rapping, drinking: he had some pretty good smoke on him, too. . . ."

Lee, who was practical about these things, held onto the joint long enough to get in three tokes before passing it to Jim, who took his one.

Frank got it now, took a deep drag, and coughed, and staggered. From the shaking floor, the record player skipped.

Phil, lighting the second joint, looked up sharply.

Grimacing and shaking his head, Frank stiff-armed the joint toward Sam. "He said he was . . ." and coughed again; and stepped away—". . . said he was staying in a commune down there. It was about five o'clock in the morning; and he asked if I . . ." He coughed some more, brought the back of his hand to his mouth, noticed the joint still pincered in his fingers, and took another toke.

Mouth clamped, he shoved it toward Sam again, who got it this time.

". . . asked . . . if . . . I . . . wanted . . . to . . . crash . . ." Frank mouthed; little smoke puffs dribbled from his mouth each word. " . . . to crash . . . at . . . this commune of his . . . on Fifth Street . . . well . . . let . . . me . . . tell . . . you . . . it was . . . a fucking . . ." Smoke exploded, with his voice, from mouth and nostrils—"rat hole! I mean, I'd come up here—I mean, I knew he'd been living up here, even if he had been kicked out; so I figured it would be something like this. But down there . . . that Place?—that's what they called it. No lights. People sleeping all over the goddamn floor. It was filthy. I swear, when we walked in, there was somebody fucking, ten feet from the door . . . God only knows who or what. They didn't even have a goddamn lock. And he tells me people have been living in their place for *months!* I could take it for just about five minutes; then I told him, 'Nooo, baby! I gotta get out of here!' I don't care how stoned I was, I couldn't take that. A commune? It was a goddamn fucking rat hole, is what it was! People who live like that aren't people, they're rats! They should stuff it up with steel wool and tack tin over it!" He turned back to Jim to get the next joint that had come around, took a toke, and began coughing again.

Lee closed her book, twisted around to put it on the shelf, and stood up. "Hey, Chip?" she said. "I've got some stuff to do back home. I think I'll split now. Phil, thanks for dinner."

"Fine!" I didn't quite say. What I came out with was: "I guess I'll run along with you."

Phil surprised me with, "Hey, I'll walk you out to the subway," and jumped out of his chair and went to the door. "Sam, there's another joint there when you guys want it. I'll be back in a while."

"Hey," Frank said, going to the chair. "Hey, thanks, man!" He picked up the joint and the matches. "Thanks!"

"Want another swig before you go?" Sam asked, and stood up with the beer bottle.

"Yeah," Lee said, and took a drink. "Thanks."

"I could use some of that," Frank said, shaking out his match. "Smoke makes you go so fucking dry!" He puffed and handed the joint to Jim. "Gimme a swing on your bottle there."

When I finished, I handed him the bottle.

He took a drink. "Now, you gotta listen to this, man! Now, this is too fucking much! Hey, Jimmy, are you listening to this?"

"Yeah," Jimmy said. He hadn't moved from his chair. "It's great."

At the bottom of the steps, we could hear the music, still yowling.

"Sure are loud," Phil said, laughing. "Sam's a great guy, but sometimes his friends are a little overwhelming." We started to walk. "I guess that's just one of the prices you pay when you share. But *you* understand that . . ." He put his hands in his jacket pocket. It was chilly, but windless. "And they're not really so bad. I just wish they didn't drink. I don't have anything moral against it, but it just isn't my thing. And it's hard to really communicate with somebody on such a different head-line."

"It was a good dinner," I said. "Thanks for feeding us."

"It was fun to have you. Lief really likes to show the place off to visitors. January House is pretty much his baby and he's proud of it. With reason too." We reached Broadway and crossed the street. "Your commune," Phil asked. "Where exactly is it?"

I was tempted to say Fifth Street, and if the purpose of life were to leave frustrating situations with devastating lines (whose devastating significances only you are totally aware of), I would have. "Down on Second Street," I told him. "But, you know, we're friends with the people at the Place."

"What place?" Phil asked.

"The Place Sam's friend Frank was talking about, on Fifth Street. They're a pretty good bunch of people."

"And they're not rats," Lee said.

"What?" Phil asked.

"Frank was talking about the Place, where the guy you booted out of January House ended up staying."

"Oh," Phil said. "I was probably busy rolling joints and missed that. Hey, don't let something Frank said get to you. I mean, he's just a drunken poet friend of Sam's. And don't let that turn you off January House. He doesn't live there. Believe me, if he did, he'd get voted out too."

Another point against devastating lines: they only work when everybody has been paying attention to the dialogue, which, off the boards, is seldom.

At the kiosk Phil said, "Well, I gotta go back and face the hordes. Thanks for coming up. And good luck with the Heavenly Breakfast. Maybe I'll get a chance to drop by there soon."

"Good," I said. "And good luck with yours." If only from exhaustion, I meant it.

Phil smiled and shook my hand. "Good night, Chip. Good night . . . Lee?"

"Good night, Phil." Lee smiled and shook his.

We'd been standing quietly on the subway platform for perhaps three minutes when I announced, "It's *not* a commune!"

Lee glanced over.

"It's a cooperative. Or a collective, maybe. But it's not a commune."

"You're going to tell them what to call themselves?"

"Then if January House *is* a commune," I said, "the Heavenly Breakfast is *not*."

"What would you suggest, then?" Lee suggested: "Crash pad? Den of iniquity? Perhaps rat hole. . . ?"

"Look," I said. "I wouldn't be all that anxious to live at the Place myself. Neither would you, probably. Not if the choice is between there and the Breakfast. I like to read and eat. And in winter that's a little hard without lights and gas. But the point is, there's a lot more in common between the Place and the Breakfast than there is between either one and January House. The Place and the Breakfast are the same kind of . . . social organization. They organize the same kinds of social space. January House is a different kind. I mean, I haven't had a meal with that large an *object*—that dining room table!—between me and the people I was eating with in I don't know *how* long!"

"We have a table," Lee said, "but we try not to let it come between people who are eating together . . . ?"

"Yeah!"

The local came; we were waiting for the express.

"'. . . the Security of the Nuclear Family,' my ass! If you've got singles and more or less monogamous couples 'who might as well be married,' living in their own little cells, each with a door they can close, you're not doing very much to the goddamn nuclear family! That's a *boarding*house up there, where the people who can't cook have to do it in spite of the ones who can!"

Somebody in a dark overcoat passed, looked, looked away.

"Lee, they *are* good people," I said. "Aren't they?"

"Anyone is a good person in the proper situation," Lee said, "if they can stand living in it. Or you don't strain them. They have good grass."

"It's ours," I said. "Grendahl sold it to Phil at the bookstore last week."

"I recognized it," Lee said. "But I didn't want to be presumptuous."

"Lee," I said, "it has been noted before: as the present slips into the past, what was, when present, a raging controversy, is revealed, when past, as the dispute between medieval theologians arguing whether twelve or twenty-four angels can dance on the head of a pin. And we review in wonder and despair: over this, people were beheaded, wars were fought, prelates excommunicated, and national boundaries realigned?"

"Didn't you write something like that in one of the books of yours they had on the back shelf?"

"Yeah." I said. "Nevertheless, I have been forced to consider the possibility this evening that capitalism—"

"Oh, come *on!*" Lee said.

"—a system that forces the greatest wealth to the strongest, cleverest, or luckiest—and Socialism—a system that forces wealth apart in equal shares—are perhaps two sides of such an argument. The future may well decide that their shared inadequacy is that neither makes any changes in those variables—the actual spaces and objects between people—that govern the equations of community and communion which, when all is said, if not done, determine how well *any* system, from dictatorship to anarchy, will work, as well as what strength subsystems will be needed to enforce it."

"Whereas," Lee said in a voice it took me a moment to realize mimicked mine, "we at the Breakfast and the Place, and the type of commune they represent, *have* adjusted these variables. . . ?"

"If ever so slightly," I said. "If we don't, the population explosion will, you know. We stand on the brink of tomorrow."

"You," Lee said, as the express came in, "are higher than *I* am."

24

I mentioned selling a story?

The morning after the visit to January House, Judy brought a postcard upstairs. It was from my agent: the check was in his office. I went uptown to get it.

George Nisbaum, one of my agent's writers, who was in the office, got to talking with me. When he learned I was "living with a group of hippies in the East Village," he was fascinated. What he wanted to know, finally, was whether I thought his own fifteen-year-old would be happy in such a place.

"I've never met your son," I said. "But from what I know of most fifteen-year-olds in the face of that much novelty, he'd probably love it."

He wanted to know about the younger people there.

Since Judy was currently the youngest living with

us, I told him about her, her speeding, her tales of home, her life with us.

He was appalled.

He was also, sincerely, concerned.

I tried to explain that, granted her situation, I could think of no better place for her than the Breakfast. People there liked her; she could talk with them; she had good food, a place to sleep; people would remind her to take her contraceptive pill in the morning; people could advise her to stay out of some of the more ridiculous dope situations she often contemplated— advice she usually took. In short, people there took as much care of her as she could accept.

Didn't we feel, George asked, anyone among us, that we must, if "her parents can do nothing with her" (the phrase is in my second notebook at the head of a list of phrases culled from our conversation), feel "a moral responsibility to get her to the police—well, maybe not to police; but to a minister; or a social worker; or maybe a psychiatrist?"

I said I didn't see the point. Any laws she'd broken, I didn't approve of anyway, so why the police? She wasn't in any particular spiritual crisis, so why a minister? Nor was she nuts. A psychiatrist?

As George talked, I realized he had no picture of Judy as an individual; nor did he have any understanding of the way her particular sort of tortured precision ("You say she's intelligent; that means, at least, there's hope for her." [phrase six]) reacts to socially usurped authority: with rage at its presumption, terror at its inconsistencies.

I walked back down to the Breakfast with my fifteen dollar check, disturbed. And appalled.

I kept reviewing the evening's conversations at January House, the morning conversation with George. I couldn't talk about life at the Heavenly Breakfast without talking about drugs and sex. Yet I couldn't mention either without their falling into value matrices set up by other people which precluded what I really wanted to discuss: the texture and affectivity of life lived humanely, day by day.

On the next page of the notebook, this entry from that afternoon (jotted while I sat on the curb at Twentieth Street and Park Avenue South—across the page from a shopping list: leg of lamb, 3 pkgs black-eyed peas, 3 heads romaine, radishes if Mr. Simon has them, cake flour [10 lbs]):

> Our culture sees anyone at an economic, social, or psychological vortex as a figure of despair. Despair informs all social dealings with them. It is impossible to show this despair is part of society's own perspective—unless you can convince people not as society but as individuals to come much, much closer; society wastes so much ability to reason, so much ability to laugh. Before laughter and reason, despair vanishes.

After so many years, honestly, I am not sure what I was trying to clarify or preserve for myself on the gray, cold, crowded noon, sitting on that curbstone. But that is my memory of the moment, and the documentation that remains.

25

Dave stood up in the bathtub (hips, fingers, knees: waterfalls); Dominiq said, "You want this?" and handed him a towel on her way into the back. Dave climbed out, supporting himself on Snipper's naked shoulder (Snipper was cutting onions), swabbing his head.

"Don't," Reema said, "splatter the stove while I'm cooking."

"Yeah, okay." Dave gave another swab at Snipper's bony back where water had run down from his hand. "Hey," he said, toweling at his chest and belly, "has anyone seen any of the people from the Place recently?"

"I saw Eddy spare-changing over in the West Village," Anne said. "I was coming out of the NYU library and we talked some in the square. We didn't say much, though; it was cold."

"I'm going around to the Place and ask them over this evening. Then I'll pick up about eight pounds of chopped meat and make chili—that should go with your half-ton of salad there," looking over Reema's shoulder.

"I'll go with you," I said.

Lee and Judy volunteered too.

Dave put on his pants, his boots, and took one of the army jackets from the nail, slid his bare arms down the sleeves, and zipped up over his chest.

Judy, Lee, and me followed him downstairs.

We walked up Avenue B, turned down Fourth Street by the schoolyard, and turned up the alley, aglitter with broken glass.

At the Place's building, Dave went down the steps, pushed open the first door, and stopped before the second. "Hey," he called back. "It's locked!"

Judy went down, and I went down after her.

Two big stainless-steel eyes, one screwed into the rotted wood of the jamb, the other in the door, were secured with a long-hasped padlock. "Lemme see." I pushed forward.

The door was loose enough so I could open it maybe three-quarters of an inch.

I put my eye to the crack.

The boards were still across the window; but there was no table. In dim winter light I could see gray board flooring. "It looks like the place has been stripped."

From the street Lee called: "What's that over there?"

Wondering, we went back out.

"Is that *Riley's* truck?" Lee started along the parked cars. We followed.

The van was gone. So were the tires.

One of the axle hubs was on the curb so that the whole cab tilted.

There was only a triangle of glass in the windshield frame, shattered, sagging, and curled across the hood like a wave, frozen in breaking. The cab, set on fire either before or after it had been stripped, was dull black.

Dave scratched his head. "Naw . . ." he said. "You can't be sure about it in that condition. It might be just any truck . . ."

There was a bodega about three doors away. Suddenly I got an idea and ran inside. "Hey," I said to the balding man behind the counter. "Do you know those people who lived down the block? They're not there anymore. Do you know what happened to them?"

He frowned at me and took his hands off the gritty marble counter to smooth his stained apron.

"One of them used to come in here almost every day and buy a couple of packs of Coca-Cola—long hair, barefoot most of the time? Even when it was cold?"

"Ohhhh!" the man said and put his hands back. "Oh, yeah. Them. They no good. The police come. They break all that shit up."

"When?" I asked.

"Two, three days ago. They no good at all. They got

93

dope; they got these colored guys in there. And these young girls. They no good."

"Jesus Christ!" I said.

Lee opened the door. "It *is* Riley's truck! Come on out and look!"

"Um . . . thanks," I said to the proprietor and went out.

I followed Lee around to the far side of the cab. Dave was regarding the charred door.

On the matt soot, one blotch-shaped area, up near the window, glistened with blisters. From it, straight down, ran lines of the same texture that stopped at a piece of ribbing and, a little farther on, started down again to the fender.

Judy asked, "Is that the place where those high-school kids out in the country . . . ?"

I reached up and touched a flaky crater where a bubble had broken. It crackled.

Pretty low, we walked back to the Breakfast.

26

The editor who had bought my story was named Sal Orlac. I'd met him a few times before. I went up to see him about a couple of minor changes I wanted to make in the text. We spent the afternoon talking about nothing in particular but had a good time. I'd heard about a small experimental theater club a few blocks from the Breakfast. Sal said it sounded interesting, and his wife, Lois, would be particularly intrigued.

Why don't we go? I said. And why didn't they stop by the Breakfast first for some wine, some smoke, some talk, before we went.

Fine.

27

I opened the door to the icebox, shook my head at Joey's bottles of peach wine, and took out the gallon of Chablis. "Hey," I said, to no one in particular, "some friends of mine are coming down this evening. The guy I sold the story to, and his wife. . . . We'll be here for a couple of hours; then we're going over to that theater club on Fourth."

I was a little surprised when Dave came up to me a minute or two later and began asking me all sorts of questions: Where did they work; how old were they; how long had I known them; was I sure they smoked? From his tone of voice I could tell he wasn't happy at the prospect of their visit.

I asked him why he was so worried.

He gave me lots of answers, most of them pretty confused, all of them uncomfortable. Basically—and the provinciality was a little surprising coming from someone I felt I knew as well as I knew Dave—he felt that because they were married, lived in Brooklyn, were on the far side of thirty, and had nine-to-five jobs, they were *a priori* not to be trusted. "But," he said, "I mean, if they're *your* friends, Chip . . . and you say they're good people. And you *know* them . . ."

Dave was the only one who seemed to feel that

way, though. Most of the others were as surprised by his feelings as I was.

At six o'clock there was a knock.

Reema answered.

Sal came in: he had on a dark overcoat, a blue suit under that, and black-framed glasses. Lois, under a tan coat, had on an orange dress.

Snipper, who had just finished a bath and was fitting the enameled cover over the tub, said hello and suggested they take off their shoes.

"Oh, I like that!" Lois said, and gave out her electric laugh that brought me and Lee from the back room.

People got introduced.

Dave, before the fact, was all smiles and curiosity.

Grendahl had been building a Rube Goldberg waterpipe out of miniature lengths of stainless-steel plumbing fixtures all afternoon on the red-checked table.

Sal, loosening his pale blue tie, walked over to examine it. "I'm afraid to guess what it is," he told Grendahl. "Is there any chance of us trying it out, though?"

"Sure! Why, sure, man!" Grendahl declared, and bounced over to the cabinet where the current smoke was kept. "Why, sure! What a great idea!"

It was a fun evening.

We all sat on the floor—Sal and Lois leaning against the john wall—on cushions and stuff. They were curious; some of the answers they got probably surprised them. But they managed to question in ways that could only flatter. For a little while Dave would come over, stand around, then drift away. Finally, even he was drawn in. Paranoid as he had been at the prospect of invaders from the square world, he became (through much the same process by which the white Southern matron becomes, once the black man is, all exclusion tactics having failed, *in* the living room, hospitality's exemplar) the *most* cordial, the *most* genial, the *most* gregarious among us.

On the narrow, chill stairs, as we were leaving for the play, Lois said to me, "I don't think I've ever been put so at ease so quickly by people who were strangers a couple of hours ago, ever before in my life!" I smiled and couldn't help thinking of Lee's and my visit to January House.

"You've got a pretty amazing bunch there," Sal said, nodding.

"We try," I said, grinning, just modest as hell.

The play was forgettable.

"Let us buy you a couple of drinks," Lois said as we came out of the theater, "and try to forget."

"Fine by me," I said. "There's a bar."

"Onward, ever onward," Sal said.

At the counter, conversation drifted back to the Breakfast. They praised the socializing qualities of pot, were tickled at Grendahl's pride in his waterpipe, concerned over Snipper's lost novel: "He's a hell of a bright kid," Sal said. "If he finds it, I'd like to take a look at it. You never know . . ." They told me they'd first tried grass just six months ago in some tentative experiments with friends. After much soul-searching, they had decided it was a Good Thing. "I mean," Sal explained, "I don't think you can compare it to the dangerous drugs, like heroin and acid."

"And of course," Lois added (this was February 1968), "everybody does."

"Well," I said, "don't knock heroin and acid till you've tried them enough times to be able to tell a good taste from a bad one."

"No no no no," Sal said as though it were one word. "I mean, I don't think anyone can really morally support the use of dangerous drugs."

"I don't see why heroin shouldn't be as socially acceptable a drug as alcohol," I said.

Sal thought that was funny.

Lois, though, detected something serious. "Seriously," she said, "a couple of blocks away from where

97

we live in Brooklyn, there's a luncheonette where a lot
of junkies hang out. All you have to do is go look at
them: they can hardly stand up. And I'm not even
talking about who's responsible for half, or more than
half, of the robberies that go on in our neighborhood."

"You like a bottle of wine with dinner, or a couple
of drinks before it," I said. "But you don't judge alcohol by the guys curled up in the doorways around
their bottles all up and down Third Avenue," and realized, as I said it, I'd taken the first steps in a sopho-
moric argument I'd sworn never to get into again back
when I was twenty. "Besides," I said, taking the second step, "acid isn't heroin and heroin isn't acid," and
resolved to keep my mouth shut—even if they *did*
think that was my point.

"Well," Sal was saying, "I just don't think I person-
ally would want to try something like acid. I mean,
from what I've heard and read. Of course, I may not
be being fair—"

"Hey," Lois said, over my shoulder. "Come on, tell
us: what's your favorite drug?"

"If you want to know," I said "heroin. But Alka-
Seltzer runs it a close second . . ." I made a balance
with my hands above the bar, which wavered. "Or cocaine."

"You mean," Sal exclaimed with the zany, if dated,
delight that the first victim of the banana-skin hoax
years back must have felt on hearing the one about
smoking the peel scrapings, "if you take a whole bottle or so of Alka-Seltzer, you'll get high?"

"One or two tablets," I said, "keeps me feeling good
three, four hours at a time. But you shouldn't do too
much of it over an extended period. You can get rup-
tured capillaries; which is not fun."

I saw Lois, who I knew from the conversation had
been reading *Drugs and the Mind*, contemplate saying something about cocaine and perforated septa. Instead, though, she decided on, "I suppose I've always

98

sort of liked all those little bubbles myself. Mmmmmm . . . Alka-Seltzer?" She glanced at Sal.

"Don't knock it," I said. "It beats peach wine, and you just spent an hour talking to one of *those* back at the Breakfast."

Then I decided, since we were on neutral territory, to change the subject. I said something about the play; they leaped at the topic. Soon as they did, I found myself thinking: a bar? With a government license to dispense and tax alcohol? For money? Neutral territory, my left nut!

All Dave's provinciality of the afternoon came to roll around under my tongue while off the top slipped commonplaces about the evening's two badly performed one-acters.

"I really *do* like the Heavenly Breakfast," Lois said when we left. "Wasn't that amazing, Sal? The way they made us so quickly a part of everything?"

He nodded, smiling. "I hope you invite us back. Say, why don't you come around to the office and let Mr. Simon and Mr. Schuster buy you some lunch—say, next Thursday, around twelve?"

"Thanks!" I said. "Sure."

And did. And ate up several dollars worth of mussels, *veau roulade*, and strawberry torte, with *café filtre*. Being seated in the back because I came in sans tie didn't bother me (nor probably Sal) a bit.

But Sal's conversation about drugs (the subject came up again, of course), as well as George Nisbaum's about Judy's speeding, returned and rehearsed themselves in memory over the next months . . . five times? A dozen times? Fifty?

28

In the last pages of my third notebook, among the entries made at the beginning of spring, are these that I wrote sitting on the stoop in front of the Heavenly Breakfast while I watched the firemen lounging in front of the firehouse across the street:

Heard this morning, from Billy, that Judy, three months pregnant, was found dead last night in a hallway on the top floor of a building on Ninth Street. She was in a state of malnutrition, had apparently O.D.'d and was probably left there by the people she was with.

A policeman? A minister? A psychiatrist?

Would they have helped her, or only quickened the process she had committed herself to because, perhaps, of its inevitable end?

But the above is a lie.

I write it because earlier this afternoon I went up to the Met, determined to do something with this second balmy mid-March day. Judy, whom we haven't seen for two months, was in the bookshop examining the postcards of Flemish paintings.

"Hi!" I said.

She looked, and for a moment I thought she didn't recognize me; and for the next, thought I'd mistaken her for someone else.

But it was Judy. She's a lot thinner. While we talked, she told me she'd given up speed, entirely. "I'm not on anything," she said. "I read Spinoza now," and she gave a little laugh. "That's supposed to be a predictable replacement for Kierkegaard."

Was she living at home? I wanted to know.

No, she was sharing a place in Brooklyn with two other girls. In fact, she was taking art classes at the Brooklyn Museum. She had come to see the rooms of Early American furniture; and I learned more than I could possibly want to know about Austin and Wright rockers. Is her mind duller? Or is it simply its hysterical edge that has gone? She is certainly happier, surer of herself.

But the above, of course, is a lie too.

These are fictional endings for stories George Nisbaum would write and Sal Orlac would publish, both thinking themselves highly moral men.

Recognize them for aesthetically manipulated lies when they occur in fiction.

More important, recognize them for the same thing when they occur, as they do, in life. They are products of the same process that for so long produced an American fiction in which all abortion ended in death, all female adultery in divorce.

When I went upstairs to the Breakfast, Judy, sitting at the table, closed the book she was reading on her forefinger.

"Hey," I said, "listen to something I just wrote, will you?"

When I'd finished, she sat for a while, looking at the light from the window across the Indian print Reema had hung on the wall. "You haven't got it," she said at last. "But you're getting there . . . at something I've been trying to tell my mother for two years now. Of course, I don't think she'll get it, no matter how it's put. But I have to keep trying to say it to her in my own way." She frowned. "And you have to keep trying to say it in yours." Then she went back to her place in the (Spinoza) *Tractatus.*

101

29

As winter had come, advancing then retreating, so came spring. A few days later it was back in the twenties.

Living with Reema over months at the Breakfast, I'd come to think of her as one of the most commonsensical and level-headed people there. For the bulk of the winter we had all been fairly house-bound. So it wasn't surprising that she decided to get a job.

She'd been a waitress in San Francisco. She thought she would like waitress work in New York. A friend of Little Dave's said he could get her a job in a restaurant on Fifth Avenue. She went up to see them; the job was hers. They would provide her uniform. She would have to buy waitress shoes, though.

"It'll be good to spend some time out of here," she told us.

"Why do you want to do that?" Dave asked.

"I just want to contribute something," she said. "I want to be able to bring some money in."

"You don't have to." Dave suddenly picked her up in his arms. "Nobody's hurting for bread. You want some money—even just to hold—tell me."

"Contribute something!" I said. "You work hard as anybody else around here—harder."

"That's another thing—" Reema said from above us all. "Come on, Dave. Put me down."

He did.

"I've hardly been outdoors since that time we all

went to the country. I want to look at some new walls. I want to see some new people. Give me some money to buy shoes. In fact, why don't you come on up with me to get them?"

"All right," Dave said. "Sure, I'll go with you."

"Does anybody else want to come?" Reema asked.

"Okay," I said. "Me too."

The three of us took the subway uptown. As we got out at our station, I noticed Reema looked very uncomfortable. "You all right?" I asked.

"The people," she said. "Look at the people walking around; don't they seem so . . . ?" Then she just shrugged.

It was Saturday. Cold as it was, the stores were still crowded. We picked a big shoe store near the restaurant.

We waited outside while she went off between the plate-glass windows. She was wearing tennis sneakers with no socks. Her blue raincoat, which she'd had dry-cleaned for the job interview, winked out behind the glare on the glass doors.

She was gone a long time.

I had on somebody else's army jacket and the zipper didn't work. Dave wore one of those kapok-filled red jackets. Only there was a foot-long tear beneath the arm and he had no shirt on under it.

"Damn," I said through white breath. "Maybe we should go in."

Which is when she came out.

She took two steps, put one hand against the display glass, then ran forward.

I caught her.

Dave caught us both.

She was crying, and taking very big breaths, which must have hurt at that temperature.

"What's . . . what's the matter?" Dave asked, over my shoulder; first he tried to smile, then didn't, and just squeezed.

She looked up, still crying, her red hair all over her face.

I pushed it aside. She caught her breath, and when I stepped back a little, I saw she'd put her hand in the tear of Dave's jacket. She leaned her face against his red nylon. "Nobody . . . nobody would *look* at me!" she got out. "Nobody in the fucking store would look at me! I saw the shoes I wanted and I couldn't get anybody to wait on me. Then finally one man just turned and snapped at me, 'All right! What do *you* want?' I hadn't done anything to him! I didn't."

We held her while she cried some more and people passing looked or didn't look.

While we walked back to the subway stop, I remembered what Dave had said to me on my third day at the Breakfast, about getting too dependent on the communal interaction. I wanted to ask if that's what he'd meant, but it didn't seem the time. By the time we got home, I'd forgotten it.

The next day, alone, Reema went to a different shoe store and got her shoes. After her first day on the job, I asked her how she liked it.

"The people I work with are pretty nice. Not as nice as here . . . but I like them." She leaned back against the edge of the tub cover. "But getting there . . . Lord, is it cold!"

30

Whoever had our apartment before Dave rented it managed to leave owing Con Edison some incredible amount of money. The Breakfast had its own account. But every six weeks or so, the electric company would send somebody around looking for the previous tenants. Once Dave happened to answer the door naked. After about ten seconds, the Con Ed man got flustered and left. Dave decided this was a good way to get rid of people he didn't want to see and took to answering the door naked whenever possible on the theory that anyone who was upset by it was probably someone he didn't want to talk to anyway. I just thought it was affected.

"*I'll* get it this time," I said, and got there while Dave was still getting off his pants, hopping around on one foot. I tugged the door open and looked out. "Yeah?"

Out in the dim hall I made out a slouching figure. His scuffed engineer boots were run over at the sides and there was a heavy chain around the right one. His hair was dark and stringy. He looked Puerto Rican. His jeans, that black-blue denim gets when it's really raunchy, hung low on a belly swirled with dark hair. His chest was bald. His hands and arms were dirty as a mechanic's. In the opening of his vest hung loops and loops of chains. At least one was a dog's choke collar. On another was a German cross. He had a braided piece of rawhide around his upper

arm, tight enough to crease the skin. Sewn an inch
left and low on his crotch was a soiled yellow ankh.
"The Heavenly Breakfast, huh?"

"What?" I asked. "Oh, yeah."

"Who is it?" Dave said, coming out (naked) behind
me. I stepped forward to make room for him.

And got a chill.

Halfway down the steps, a black guy in the same
getup was leaning against the banister, his arms
folded. A third, with lank blond hair down a boney
back, sat down on the bottom of the landing.

The one who'd knocked said, "You guys had any
trouble around here?"

"Pardon?" Dave said.

The guy talking wasn't fazed by Dave's nakedness
at all. The ones on the stair didn't even look. "Trouble.
You know, anybody giving you any shit: your landlord,
uptight neighbors, anybody like that?"

"No," Dave said.

"You guys are dealing," he didn't ask. "You have
any shit with stool pigeons—" was the word he really
used—"or somebody you think is into the narcs, you
come tell us about it, huh? We whipped ass on a couple of motherfuckers already that weren't doing right
by people. You get anybody giving you a hard time,
you just let us know. You know where we are?"

"A good question," Dave said. "Just where *are* you
guys?"

"Eleventh Street—three-thirty-four." Then he turned
and clumped down the steps, the others falling
in with him. At the bottom, the grubby, jangling trio
wheeled around the rickety newel and tramped away.

"That," Dave said as we went back inside, "is too
fucking weird." He picked up his pants from the table
and slipped one leg into the shabby purple corduroy.

"You are the only person I know," Reema said, "who
takes his pants off before answering the door, then

comes back inside to put them on. What was that all about?"

We told them.

"Jesus," Grendahl said. "I'd just as soon leave that kind of vendetta shit alone. It sounds too weighty for me." ("Heavy" was to make its way in from California in the next three months.) "Besides, we don't have these kinds of problems—knock on wood."

"I think you're right," Dave said. "The vendetta business puts the whole thing on a level I'd be just as happy staying away from."

"At least," I said, "it's nice to know somebody cares."

"I think," Grendahl said, "I'd be just as happy if they didn't."

"Three-thirty-four," Little Dave said, looking up from his drawing board a moment, "is Phyllis' old building."

31

Three-thirty-two was a rubble-strewn lot. Three-thirty-six was just a shell, halfway through demolition.

There was tin over the ground-floor windows of the building in between. At the top of cracked terra-cotta-colored steps, the door not only had no lock, it had no doorknob. The street lamp on the corner wasn't working. Things were very dark inside.

I pushed into the chilly, fetid hallway. Behind the door to the apartment with the tinned-over windows, a radio played WPAT-style Muzak. I wondered how long ago Phyllis had left here. Half the mailboxes had no doors.

At the end of the hallway on the second floor, one door was padlocked, recalling the Place. But on the fourth, someone had taken an aerosol can of black paint and tried to cross out a red swastika, wide as the door it was painted on. It was still pretty visible.

I thought about going away.

A shrill voice complained loudly behind one of the walls.

I took a breath; and knocked.

The door jerked open about half an inch. "What?"

"Hello . . ." I said. "Um . . . I just came by to say hello."

"What?" but this time with a rising instead of a falling inflection.

"I'm from the Heavenly Breakfast, on Second Street," I said. "Some of you guys came by to see us and be neighborly; so I thought I'd return the visit."

"Oh . . ." He opened the door about a foot and stepped back. Behind him, the walls were the color of polluted sky. I stepped in. In another room, a woman and a man argued raucously. "Well, then . . . Hello." The guy who'd opened the door rubbed his stomach the way someone else who'd just woken up might rub his eyes. His hand hit the long chains hanging from his neck and jangled them.

On a bare mattress a black girl in leather pants, no shirt, and nap-short hair sat cross-legged. A brown guy beside her, whose coarse curls, from the outside of his shoulders to his head, made a rounded pyramid, had an arm around her. She looked unhappy. He looked solicitous.

In the other room, the harsh woman-voice wound its obstacle course through consonant-studded invectives.

Six other guys sat or stood around the room.

"Make yourself at home, I guess," the guy who'd

108

opened the door said in a friendly enough way, even though I was in already. Then he turned, shrugged, and walked out of the room.

An eight-foot skull and crossbones had been painted over one wall, in red and black, by someone who painted pretty well, too. Hooked by bent nails to another wall were the springs from a double bed. From them hung some leather straps, a few chains, a pair of handcuffs, and some frayed gray lengths of clothesline. There were gates on the windows, but neither shades nor curtains.

"Hey," somebody said from the end of the room.

I looked.

"How you been doing?" He got up from the chair he'd been sitting on (astraddle, backwards, arms folded on the backrest) and ambled toward me, grinning. His yellow hair was as short as the girl's, his skimpy blond beard almost the same length. Shirtless (but without chains), he had what looked like a studded leather dog collar around his neck. He slid his hands under the waist of his beltless jeans, thumbs outside. About a foot of the seam down his right leg was torn so that the side of his white knee flashed at each step.

"Hello." I tried to figure out why he thought he knew me. He was a muscular little guy who didn't come up to my chin. Then I got a flash: "Riley . . . ?"

He stuck out his hammy hand, dirty as when I'd first met him. "Good to see you, man! What you guys been doing, huh?"

"Eh . . . not much!" Surprised, I shook. "Making music. Have you been here since the Place got closed up?"

"Just about. Had a few days on the street. I don't have my truck anymore."

"Yeah," I said. "I saw it."

"Ain't that a bitch? I wish I'd known about here, back when the Place was havin' all its hassles.

There'd been some asses whipped. How're things at the Breakfast? I'd like to see you guys again."

"Uh . . . sure," I said. "You should come on by." I looked around the room. There was one unfrosted light bulb in the ceiling fixture, whose yellow glare blackened the window glass behind the bars.

"You up here for business?" Riley asked. "You got any hassles over at the Breakfast, man? 'Cause that's what we take care of, motherfucker! You make music? Well, we whip ass. That's what we do." He grinned.

"No," I said. "No, everything's cool with us. Really. I just was curious to see the setup here. I'm just being nosey."

"Naw," Riley said. "You're bein' friendly. I know: you guys down there are just friendly guys. That's real good, man." He reached up to pat my shoulder. "That's good."

"Is anybody else here from the Place?"

"Naw. Just me. Eddy used to come by sometimes. But I don't know where the pimply-assed bastard is now. Maybe San Francisco. He always talked about San Francisco. I'd like to see him again."

In the other room the vituperation changed pitch. Riley glanced at the door. When he looked back, he had a sort of grimace on his face. "You know, man"— his hand rested on my shoulder—"this is really sort of a funny time to visit—"

"I know, it is sort of late—"

"Naw," Riley said. "Naw, that ain't it," and glanced again at the door. "We just been goin' through some changes around here, you know? Family problems. I really would like to see you guys again. Come on by again sometime soon, huh?"

"Yeah," I said. "And you come by to see us. . . ."

Inside, the curses screeched on.

"Sure," Riley said. "Sure, that'd be real nice."

I left. It was four o'clock in the morning.

32

"Phyllis made it sound weird," Little Dave said, leaning against the table, "but your description puts it beyond the pale!"

"Well," I said, "it was interesting. And I sort of like Riley."

The sun was a slash of red bronze across the upper half of the grimy pane.

"Me too," Lee said. "But you have to admit, all that paraphernalia is pretty bizarre. *Bed* springs?"

"I don't know," I said. "Of all the communes I've encountered, that's the one I'd like to write the novel about."

"Does that whole trip really interest you?" Lee asked.

"I never claimed to be a paragon of normal desire—"

"I," she said, "am going to bed. It's sunrise already."

"I," I said, "am going to sit here and mull."

Little Dave sighed, went back to the corner, and picked up his sketchbook. I got my notebook, sat at the table gnawing my eraser for a long time, every once in a while looking up, while spring light slanted through the room like summer, alive with motes.

Once Dominiq came out sleepily, stepped over the coil of amplifier cables, came over to me, hugged me so that my face slipped between her brown breasts and I felt her warm belly on my chest; then she laughed, and went to sit on the john. After she'd gone back inside, a couple of other people woke up, came out.

Someone ran water in the teakettle.

Somebody else put some bacon up. The fat began its complaint to the hot skillet.

People spoke softly.

A few minutes later, I went and got into bed with Lee. Riley never came by. I never went back.

I never saw any of them, not even on the street, again.

33
───────────────────────────────

At March-end, the Heavenly Breakfast, rock band and commune, disbanded. To describe how, let me temporarily skip several years and several thousand miles. . . .

I'd been living in San Francisco for a while. About a month back, a magazine in New York had asked me for an article on communes. I had found these notebooks and, browsing, invaded my memories—I had typed perhaps twenty-five pages of reminiscences already. I'd also tried to analyze the communal process formally, to define what it was I saw at the Heavenly Breakfast on Second Street that was the same at the Place on Fifth; at Summer, when they came in from New Jersey; or even the same with Phyllis' rambunctious onetime neighbors; also, why I could say, whether it worked for good or ill at any of these places, at a place like January House it was absent.

But no social process is exhausted by simple description.

One can only fix recognizable emblems that, hopefully, imply the fuller texture. I have a note on a linguistic phenomenon: living as constantly close as one does in a communal situation, almost all exchanges are between "I" and "you." "We" was a term "we" at the Breakfast, at any rate, only used with visitors.

Since there was no permanent, externally agreed-on social organization structure, it's accurate to say that everything that happens in the commune was because of "your" or "my" whim. But "you" and "I" lived so close that the effect of "your" whim on "me" or "my" whim on "you" was immediately apparent. And there was no way to avoid responsibility for it. I worked, I ate, I bathed, I shit, I fucked, I went to sleep, and I woke up in the same room with you. There were no rooms you were not in. In that situation, it is impossible for me to allow you to do more work than you're comfortable doing, as you look around and see what is to be done; as you see what I'm doing; or what she or he is doing; or as you decide what, by whim, you feel like doing. That outraged hostility you experience when you have been socially mistreated, with which you can freeze a whole room of strangers, much less friends, just by walking into it in the right mood, I cannot tolerate when I am sleeping in the same bed you're balling in, when I'm balling in the same bed she's sleeping in, when she sits down on a toilet seat he's just left warm, when he's leaning against your leg while he eats, when I can feel your back muscles moving against mine while you eat.

I do not believe in telepathy. I know your feelings through my eyes, through my ears. The information comes via light and sound: the square of the distance intervening between us must be a diminishing factor in how much information and energy crosses from me to you and back. But when you and I live *so* closely

113

that touch and smell are suddenly half of what we communicate, new laws govern the interchanges as different as strong and weak particle interactions.

This was about the point in the article I was at when Lee called me up one afternoon. She, Little Dave, and their three-month-old son were visiting San Francisco for several weeks. They were staying in a commune on Oak Street. She told me that Dominiq, who was studying art at Chanard in L.A., had come up with an experimental opera group. Would I like to go see the show with them? Reema, who was also in San Francisco, with her year-old kid, was coming.

Sure, I said. I'd see them at the community center where the performance was being held Saturday.

That evening Snipper knocked on my door. He'd hitchhiked in from Denver. His new group had just cut its first album. He presented me with a copy, bowed, and said, "Could I please fall out somewhere? I am bushed!"

He stayed with me a couple of days. That Saturday we all took off for the community center.

After the show (a colorful happening/dance/musical, with lots of wire-form animals moved by singers around a Styrofoam-and-Saran-Wrap Garden of Eden, while the forces of light—Johnny Appleseed, played by Dominiq in clown-face—battled the forces of darkness—Dracula, played by a thin, vital woman in black tights and silver face-paint—before the bleachers of the community-center gymnasium) when we were reconnoitering with Reema, Lee, and Little Dave, across the crowd we suddenly recognized Billy and Janice. With them was (Big) Dave—just back from Hawaii, it turned out. Everybody came over to my place; and for the first time in five years ten of us were in the same room again.

We drank wine, reminisced, and had a fine old time. "It's too bad Grendahl's not here," Dominiq said.

"Then we'd have practically everybody. When does he get out?"

"He's still got a year," Dave said. "When are they gonna make grass legal?"

"Hey," Snipper said. "Why don't you break out your article?"

"Ah, yes," said Little Dave. "I want to see what this looks like!"

"It's just in note form," I said. "Recollections of a few incidents. But you can all tell me what you think of the idea." I got out the manuscript and, with re-filled wineglasses, passed it around.

"I don't want to actually read it," Snipper said, "until it's published." He had put his album on for the third time, which was fine with us. We liked it a lot. "Then I can check it out with the way *I* remember. You can say anything you want, as long as you promise you'll use my real name."

"I promise nothing," I said. "You may end up struck out of existence by a blue pencil."

Dominiq, still in her Johnny Appleseed makeup, came back from the corner where she'd been reading for the last twenty minutes. "That's odd," she said. "I was going through so many changes back then, doing so much growing, getting ready for all the things I'm into now. It was one of the most exciting times in my life!" She frowned. "All you have me doing is drifting around changing light bulbs and being sweet. . . . Don't you remember that incredible trip we took, where you and Judy and I talked for hours and hours and hours?"

I frowned. "I . . . No, I don't."

"Christ!" She struck her forehead with the heel of her hand. "One of the most important conversations in my life—where I must have done at least three years' growing up in one night: he was *intimately* involved, and he doesn't remember!" She crossed her hands over the papers on her knees. "That's life, I suppose. Well, it's nice you remember me as sweet, then. Lord knows there was enough reason to think of me otherwise." Then, leering through her opera makeup, she blew me a kiss, a parodic gesture to all things saccharine.

From the several other people who read it that night, Lee's comments are the ones I remember most clearly:

"When you first mentioned writing it, I got the feeling right off that it wasn't a good idea. Having read it, though, I may have changed my mind."

"Have I misrepresented anything?" I asked. "Do you think I've left out too much?"

"Well," she said, "you've left out an awful lot about yourself."

The others laughed. They all agreed there.

Lee moved Reema's kid over on her knee and paged through the typescript. "Here, for instance." She quoted: " 'Sex, for all practical purposes, was perpetual, never private, and polymorphous, if not perverse.' True. . . ." She smiled. "But *you* know it was a lot more interesting than that." She handed me back the *ms*. "Go ahead," she said. "Publish it." She glanced up at Little Dave.

"Yeah," he said, nodding.

Lee said, "It won't hurt anything." Then she laughed. "It might even be good."

34

At March-end, the Heavenly Breakfast got its biggest break. Basically, we had always been interested in recording rather than performing. Between the four of us in the band proper, we played thirty-six instruments; four people can play thirty-six instruments only when they have multiple-track tape recorders at their disposal. Contingent upon the pop-music boom in the mid-sixties, eight small but well-equipped recording studios had opened up over the last two years and were independently producing a number of small groups.

One of these had heard us, liked us, and had allotted us three full days' recording time with a really good engineer to put together a master tape, having approved our homemade demos.

Reema was sitting on the windowsill with one of the acoustic guitars (playing a song I'd written).

From the kitchen, Snipper's high electric notes fractured the apartment. Underneath, Lee's flute burbled, then gave to the blaring shawm. "Come on!" Dave called. "Let's get some work done!"

I shrugged at Reema, grinned, and went in to rehearse.

How to talk about Heavenly Breakfast music? It was a time measured off by music, defined by music's making. To talk about anything but the music is to distort the Heavenly Breakfast experience. (And thus I

117

suppose I have done mostly that.) Music was what we were into. Music was why we were there.

Our songs ranged from a piece of Webern brevity that Lee had written—

> If I try to thank you,
> run away—
> or I will tell you
> all the little things
> you didn't know
> I knew
> that you
> wanted
> known.

—to a four-part chromatic round lifted from the late Renaissance, *She Weepeth Sore in the Night.* We were heaviest on vocals. Dave and Snipper were our most prolific song writers. Dave's, with their beat and their progressions clawing from key to key, were perhaps the most fun to sing. Snipper's, with their zany lyrics and the clear, open arrangements they lent themselves to, were probably the most fun to hear.

The rules of thumb with which we approached our music: repeating a musical phrase the same way twice needs a hell of a better reason than *a-a-b-a* song form. Never do anything confused that can be done simple. Never do anything dull that can be done interesting.

During those last rehearsals, I kept recalling a story I'd once heard about Michelangelo: someone had once asked him, "Master, how do you judge the aesthetic composition of a sculptural work?"

"Well," replied the genius, "you take it to the top of a hill, then give it a roll. If, by the time it reaches the bottom, something has cracked off, chances are your composition's bad."

Similarly, the way to judge a recording arrangement is to take your highest-of-fi multiple-track tape and play it back through a one-and-a-half-inch speaker on a really bad transistor radio. If it's dull or muddy, your arrangement's probably bad. Rules of thumb, now. But they were learned in the instant Lee's eyes narrowed while she watched for Dave's entrance; when Dave and Snipper's voices caught at a note tossed from a guitar lead which fixed the point in the time matrix of the song so that, lead or no, it was always there: or when all my body's muscles would release together to tumble a tenor run oblique to Lee's flute. It was learned in the same way we learned how and why the spontaneous happens so well, so often, and so rewardingly, the more exacting (and the more familiar we were with the exactitudes of) the framing structure.

That Saturday's rehearsal, we finished laying recorder guide-tracks for the pieces to be taped the next day. To make full use of our time, each piece had to be practically choreographed. Tracking schedules were laid out. Little Dave was keeping notes; he would be riding with the engineer in the control booth. The songs came as melodies and words with feeling not to be underlined but to be created *by* the arrangement. In play and in work, new things grew out of the burgeoning gestalt: at a certain richness, the whole process was atomized again and each part studied and polished separately, with the hope that, on tape, when they dovetailed once again, creation would be even richer.

"Okay," Dave said sometime after eleven, "I think we've got about as much done as we can do. We tape at noon tomorrow. Go to sleep. If we don't know what we're doing by now . . ." He looked pretty tired.

So were the rest of us.

Sunday morning, we got out of bed, packed up instruments; Snipper, Lee, Dave and I, with two cases apiece; Grendahl and Little Dave and Reema came along, each lugging more. "Good luck," Joey said. "I may drop by the recording studio this afternoon and bring in a little refreshment."

"Make it Cokes." Snipper grinned and went out the door.

The studio was a reconverted warehouse on Pitt Street.

It was a chill, misty New York March and an eight-block walk. Dave and Snipper began singing in the street. Two blocks more, and we had half a dozen children running behind us, clapping to what could be clapped to, wide-eyed and laughing at Snipper's improvised lyrics.

We'd been to the studio two or three times to check out their equipment, see how we were going to set things up. It was a great plank door, with the name in wooden letters across the top. We got there five minutes to twelve.

Nailed to the door was a piece of brown paper bag on which was lettered in red Magic Marker:

DUE TO UNFORESEEN CIRCUMSTANCES WE HAVE BEEN FORCED TO SUSPEND ALL OPERATIONS. ARTISTS AFFECTED SHOULD CALL . . .

Dave put his cases down on the cracked paving. "What the fuck is *that*?"

We called, got no answer.

Lee thought of someplace else to call, where we got a very confused one.

We lugged our instruments back to the Breakfast—stopping in a bar once, at Snipper's suggestion, to call another one of the small recording studios uptown where an engineer worked who sometimes doubled in the studio we'd just left. Dave got busy signals, five times in a row.

While we drank our beers at the bar, we kept glancing at the glass door of the phone booth in the corner: then Dave got through.

After a moment he came out looking very funny. "I spoke to the secretary there," he said, frowning. "*They* officially went out of business last night at midnight; and she's just taking calls for the next day or two. She couldn't tell me why, or wouldn't, or anything about the Pitt Street studio."

Another forty-eight hours of phone calls here and there just produced more confusion. But we did learn: four other small studios in the city were suddenly, temporarily or permanently, out of business. The last call reached the engineer who was to have been working with us that Sunday we found the note:

Con Edison had changed its credit policy to the small studios and foreclosed on all eight of them, demanding immediate payment. Six of them had gone out of business. The other two were no longer small as a result. Where they had been charging thirty-five and forty dollars an hour for recording time, they were now charging eighty-five and up. Even at those prices, they still did not have a spare minute, much less a spare day.

There was a week of finagling and conniving, at the end of which we figured the guy was right. The time of the small, independent, studio-produced group in New York was over.

The closest thing we ever had to a meeting at the Heavenly Breakfast happened the next Sunday. The four of us in the group, plus half a dozen, sat around the kitchen talking.

"I don't know what to say," Snipper said, sitting on the table edge. "But I don't think it's gonna work anymore."

I sat in the chair. Lee sat on the floor. Dave was leaning against the stove, waiting for a pot of coffee to perk. "What do you want to do . . . ? Do you want to call it quits?"

I said, "We've been together just over a year, and half that year has been here. And we've made some good music. But what got us together in the first place was the fact that all those little studios were around, and pulling our kind of music out of the great void, some of them doing pretty well with it too. They're not there now. . . ."

"So you *do* want to call it quits," Snipper said, considering.

"Yeah," I said. "I do."

"We could forget the small studios," Dave said. "We could plunge right on, you know? What's wrong with hitting the big ones?"

"Because they won't give us a listen unless we've been doing ballrooms and concert tours and the whole rock-'n'-roll-star bit."

"So we go perform! What's wrong with doing it in front of an audience?"

"Nothing," I said. "If you can. I'm just not very good at it. I made a lousy enough living at it for two years to *know* I'm not very good at it, too. I have ideas, and I can realize them if I only have to get them over that six inches between me and the microphone and don't have to think about anything else. You're different, Dave. You *have* the whole theatrical thing; and you have it hard. You want to do it, you do it well, and the sort of closet music we've been making probably holds you back, if anything—"

"I've *liked* working with you guys!"

"I've liked working with you," I said.

"Aw, come on," Dave said. "Lee, you say something."

"I like making music," Lee said, "with people. For me, though, the people are the most important thing. I'd be just as happy with a chamber group, playing Telemann. Maybe even a little . . . no, I started to say 'happier.' But it would just be different. I'd like the group to go; who wouldn't? But I can't see batting my head up against a wall to sell it if there's no one to sell it to anymore."

Dave said, "If people could *hear* the music, they'd buy it!"

Lee said, "But you have to sell it to a producer first."

"Yeah, but that just means we haven't found the right—"

"I want to work alone," Snipper said. Then, after a few seconds, he said, in the open voice he would use to tell children the sky is blue: "I love you. I love our music. But I want to go on. And with no small, independent studios, we can't: not the way we have been, not with the same kind of music, not . . ."—he shrugged "—like this."

Lee said, "That whole business, with the studios' shutting down: I feel like the cat in the cartoon chasing after the bird, who runs off the edge of a cliff, doesn't realize it, and keeps running for another fifteen feet; suddenly she notices something's wrong, looks down, sees there's nothing there, turns, and starts running back; even gets about six feet—before she falls. We didn't put the cliff there. It's not our fault. But we're hanging in midair, in a way that we weren't last week."

Coffee began to perk.

Dave glanced back at the pot with folded arms, then looked at us. "I want to work in front of an audience. You're not the people to do it with." He sighed.

I felt relieved.

"Pour me a cup of that when it's ready," Snipper said. He was relieved too.

"What's going to happen to . . . ?" Lee looked around the kitchen. "I mean, what's going to happen to the . . . apartment here?" Which, I guess, was when we knew there was no more Heavenly Breakfast.

35

Next morning's mail brought another postcard from my agent: "Since you don't have a phone, it is hard to get you good news when it comes. Drop up to the office."

I did. Over a desk full of confused papers and handsome paperweights, he said, "Your last book just sold its paperback rights, and for an unusually handsome sum. Would you like some money?"

That afternoon I rented a three-room apartment on Seventh Street; there was a mattress in it already, and a chair. I figured I'd paint the walls white. Yeah, and maybe the little room where I would sleep: silver. With one wall blue. Yeah.

I walked back down to Second Street to get my stuff.

"It's a fresh pot," Little Dave said, at the stove when I walked in. "Want any?"

"Yeah."

Lee was at the table drinking some.

"What's happening?" I asked.

"Well," Lee said, "right after you left this morning, Dave took Reema out to the airport, put her on a plane to San Francisco. He is currently hitchhiking in the same direction. He said it would be more fun."

I nodded, took my cup from Little Dave, and sat down on the other side of the table. "I just rented a place on Seventh," I said. "I was going to pick up some stuff."

She nodded. "Figured you were doing something like that. Dave said I could have the apartment here. Snipper and me will stick around for a while. And anybody else who wants."

"You want to move in with me?" I asked. Which was a question I'd been contemplating all day.

"Not overly," Lee said. Which was one of the answers I'd been contemplating with it.

"Figured," I said. But I was surprised how much it annoyed me.

"You'd be impossible to live with by yourself." She smiled. "Besides, I'm not ready to leave here yet."

I nodded. Which was just admitting we were still close.

Joey, with his bottle, was in the corner, reading.

I could hear Grendahl practicing on an acoustic in the back room.

I sipped coffee, black. "You work on something a year," I said. "And it comes to nothing."

"I suppose it's not all *that* consoling to remember other people have worked on other things a lot longer and had them come to the same." She swirled tan coffee in the blue cup. "One remembers anyway. The people . . ." She looked around. "This place is going to break up fairly soon. I'll be here for a while. But not forever. Remember January House, uptown? Lief's place?"

I nodded.

"I'm just thinking what he said about making a place like this more stable. The music is something that's always with you. But the thing I'm saddest about is the commune breaking up."

"I still think Lief was thinking about a different kind of place," I said. "Maybe an essential part of communes is their impermanence. Maybe communes just break up."

"But you . . ." Lee said. "You *do* think it's a better way of life than the cooperative. You said so."

I pondered a second. "Yeah. But in the evolutionary sense. The commune is a more delicate organism than the co-op, more sensitive, more vulnerable, possibly shorter-lived. Maybe it's the compulsive desire for things to be permanent that's neurotic. After all, nothing is. Humans are an evolutionary advance over the sea turtle, even though the sea turtle is tougher, weighs more, and lives longer."

"I was thinking, at first," Lee said, "since I'm more or less in charge now, of trying to have a few organizational meetings and things. But that would make it something else. And I think I want to see how this ends, naturally. The people who've gone already have cut out with pretty good feelings." She frowned into her cup. "Tell me, what do you think about . . . this all? I mean, now that it's over?"

"About what?"

She gestured around the kitchen. "The . . . commune."

"I don't know," I said. "Without any of their disadvantages, it combines the best points of a jail, a mental hospital, a brothel—"

In the corner, Joey cracked up, so that he nearly spilled the bottle.

"Oh, come on!" Lee said. "Get out of here . . ."

"Yeah," I said. That was all I could think of to say. "Well, I'll lug my stuff on up to my place."

"You need any help getting there?" Little Dave asked.

I laughed. "I don't have any stuff to take."

"Drop by if you get hungry," Lee said. Then she laughed too. "Or if you feel like cooking."

"Sure," I said. "I will. And you drop by and see where I am."

"Sure." She smiled.

With the three notebooks jammed inside my guitar case, I went downstairs, stopped on the stoop a few seconds to look up and down the street.

Then I walked to the corner.

ABOUT THE AUTHOR

SAMUEL R. DELANY, born April Fool's Day, 1942, grew up in New York City's Harlem. His novels *Babel-17* and *The Einstein Intersection* both won Nebula Awards from the Science Fiction Writers of America, as have his short fictions *Aye, and Gomorrah* and *Time Considered as a Helix of Semi-Precious Stones* (which also took a Hugo Award during the World Science Fiction Convention at Heidelberg). His books include *The Jewels of Aptor*, *The Fall of the Towers*, *Nova*, *Driftglass* (short stories), *Dhalgren*, *Triton*, *Heavenly Breakfast* (nonfiction) and *Tales of Nevèrÿon*. With his wife, National Book Award-winning poet Marilyn Hacker, he co-edited the speculative fiction quarterly *Quark*. He also wrote, directed and edited the half-hour film *The Orchid*. In 1975 he was visiting Butler Chair Professor of English at the State University of New York at Buffalo. For the last half dozen years Delany and Hacker have lived between New York, San Francisco and London. They have one daughter.

THE IMAGINATIVE WORLDS OF
SAMUEL R. DELANY

NOVA
A passion for vengeance drives Capt. Lorq von Ray to dare what no mortal has ever done—to sail through the splintering core of a disintegrating sun. His obsession draws aimless souls into the vortex of his madness—wandering adventurers who would plug into any ship that promises escape.

DHALGREN
The sun has grown deadly. The world has gone mad, society has perished and savagery rules. All that was known is over, all that was familiar is strange and terrible. In these dying days of earth a nameless young drifter enters the city—to influence the lives of those around him.

TRITON
The human race has colonized Triton, moon of Neptune, where the ideals of universal prosperity are possible. Within this strange climate of complete utopia and certain doom, Bron Helstrom seeks passion and purpose from a gypsy woman whose wisdom and power will forever reverse his life.

TALES OF NEVÈRŸON
The world of a barbarous alien empire ruled by primal brutality, intrigue and fear. A world of bizarre paradoxes, powerful mysteries and sexual abandon. The world of Gorgik, thick-hewn mine slave whose prowess defies the mighty.

HEAVENLY BREAKFAST
A long, searching personal look back at the scenes of Samuel Delany's youthful adventures—the launching pad for the psychedelic voyages that shapes his phenomenal science fiction.

These books by Samuel Delany are all Bantam Books, available wherever paperbacks are sold.

OUT OF THIS WORLD!

That's the only way to describe Bantam's great series of science fiction classics. These space-age thrillers are filled with terror, fancy and adventure and written by America's most renowned writers of science fiction. Welcome to outer space and have a good trip!